It moved.

Very fast, oh so very fast. Shards of reflection like chromed glass inlaid in adamantine black metal. It made an incongruously soft gurgling sound as it sprang soundlessly toward Rains. The convict was unable to identify it, had never seen anything like it, except perhaps in some especially bad dreams half remembered from childhood.

In an instant it was upon him, and at that moment he would gratefully have sought comfort in his worst nightmares.

A hundred meters down the tunnel Golic and Boggs listened to their compani

ALIEN³

A L I E N ³

novelization by
ALLEN DEAN FOSTER

•

based on a screenplay by
DAVID GILER & WALTER HILL
and LARRY FERGUSON

•

story by
VINCENT WARD

WARNER BOOKS

A Time Warner Company

WARNER BOOKS EDITION

Warner Books, Inc.
1271 Avenue of the Americas
New York, N.Y. 10020

 A Time Warner Company

Printed in the United States of America

First Printing: June, 1992

10 9 8 7 6 5 4 3 2 1

With thanks to Insight Computers of Tempe, Arizona for their wonderful computers.

ADF

■ - I - ■

Bad dreams.

Funny thing about nightmares. They're like a chronically recurring disease. Mental malaria. Just when you think you've got them licked they hit you all over again, sneaking up on you when you're unprepared, when you're completely relaxed and least expect them. Not a damn thing you can do about it, either. Not a damn thing. Can't take any pills or potions, can't ask for a retroactive injection. The only cure is good sound sleep, and that just feeds the infection.

So you try not to sleep. But in deep space you don't have any choice. Avoid the cryonic chambers and the boredom on a deep-space transport will kill you. Or even worse, you'll survive, dazed and mumbling after the sacrifice of ten, twenty, thirty years of useless consciousness. A lifetime wasted gazing at gauges, seeking enlightenment in the unvarying glare of readouts of limited colors. You can read, and watch the vid, and exercise, and think of what might have been had you opted to slay the boredom with deep sleep. Not many professions where it's considered desirable to sleep on the job. Not a bad deal at all. Pay's good, and you have the chance to observe social and technological advance from a unique perspective. Postponing death does not equate with but rather mimics immortality.

Except for the nightmares. They're the inescapable downside to serving on a deep-space vessel. Normal cure is to wake up. But you can't wake up in deep sleep. The machines won't let you. It's their job to keep you under, slow down your body functions, delay awareness. Only, the engineers haven't figured out yet how to slow down dreams and their bastard cousin the nightmare. So along with your respiration and circulation your unconscious musings are similarly drawn out, lengthened, extended. A single dream can last a year, two. Or a single nightmare.

Under certain circumstances being bored to death might be the preferable alternative. But you've got no options in deep sleep. The cold, the regulated atmosphere, the needles that poke and probe according to the preset medical programs, rule your body, if not your life. When you lie down in deep sleep you surrender volition to the care of mechanicals, trusting in them, relying on them. And why not? Over the decades they've proven themselves a helluva lot more reliable than the people who designed them. Machines bear no grudges, engage in no animosity. The judgments they render are based solely on observation and analysis. Emotion is something they're not required to quantify, much less act upon.

The machine that was the *Sulaco* was doing its job. The four sleepers on board alternately dreamt and rested, speeding along their preprogrammed course coddled by the best technology civilization could devise. It kept them alive, regulated their vitals, treated momentary blips in their systems. Ripley, Hicks, Newt, even Bishop, though what was left of Bishop was easy to maintain. He was used to being turned on and off. Of the four he was the only one who didn't dream, didn't have nightmares. It was something he regretted. It seemed like such a waste of time, to sleep but not to dream. However, the designers of the advanced android series to which he belonged would have regarded dreaming as an expensive frivolity, and therefore did not apply themselves to the resolution of the problem.

Naturally no one thought to inquire of the androids what they thought of the situation.

After Bishop, who technically was part of the ship and not the crew and therefore did not count, Hicks was the worst off of the sleepers. Not because his nightmares were any more severe than those of his companions, but because the injuries he had recently suffered did not lend themselves to extended neglect. He needed the attention of a modern, full-service medical facility, of which the closest example lay another two years travel time and an enormous distance away.

Ripley had done what she could for him, leaving final diagnosis and prescription to the efficient judgment of the *Sulaco*'s medical instrumentation, but as none of the ship's medical personnel had survived the trouble on Archeron, his treatment was perforce minimal. A couple of years locked in deep sleep were not conducive to rapid healing. There was little she'd been able to do except watch him slide into protective unconsciousness and hope.

While the ship did its best his body labored to repair the damage. Slowing down his vitals helped because that likewise slowed down the spread of potential infection, but about the internal injuries he'd suffered, the ship could do nothing. He'd survived this long on determination, living off his reserves. Now he needed surgery.

Something was moving in the sleep chamber that was not a part of the ship, though in the sense that it too was wholly driven by programming it was not so very different from the cold, indifferent corridors it stalked. A single imperative inspired its relentless search, drove it mindlessly onward. Not food, for it was not hungry and did not eat. Not sex, for it had none. It was motivated solely and completely by the desire to procreate. Though organic, it was as much a machine as the computers that guided the ship, though it was possessed of a determination quite foreign to them.

More than any other terrestrial creature it resembled a horseshoe crab with a flexible tail. It advanced across the smooth floor of the sleep chamber on articulated legs fashioned of an unusually carbon-rich chiton. Its physiology was simple, straightforward, and designed to carry out but one biological function and to do that better than any comparable construction known. No machine could have done better.

Guided by senses that were a unique combination of the primitive and sophisticated, driven by an embedded imperative unequaled in any other living being, it scuttled determinedly across the chamber.

Scaling the smooth flank of the cryonic cylinder was a simple matter for something so superbly engineered. The top of the chamber was fashioned of transparent metallic glass. Within slept a small organic shape; half-formed, blond, innocent save for her nightmares, which were as sophisticated and frequently more extensive than those of the adults sleeping nearby. Eyes closed, oblivious to the horror which explored the thin dome enclosing her, she slept on.

She was not dreaming. Presently the nightmare was concrete and very real. Far better that she remained unaware of its existence.

Impatiently the thing explored the sleep cylinder, beginning at one end and working methodically up to the head. The cylinder was tight, triple-sealed, in many ways more secure than the hull of the *Sulaco* itself. Though anxious, the creature was incapable of frustration. The prospect of imminent fulfillment of its biological imperative only excited it and drove it to greater efforts. The extensible tube which protruded from its ventral side probed the unyielding transparency which shielded the helpless body on the unreachable cushions, proximity to its quarry driving the creature into a frenzy of activity.

Sliding to one side, it eventually located the nearly imperceptible line which separated the transparent dome of the cylinder from its metal base. Tiny claws drove into the minuscule crack as the incredibly powerful tail secured a purchase on the instrumentation at the head of the cylinder. The creature exerted tremendous leverage, its small body quivering with the effort. Seals were strained. The thing's effort was unforgiving, its reserves of strength inconceivable.

The lower edge of the transparent dome snapped, the metallic glass splitting parallel to the floor. A sliver of the clear material, sharp as a surgical instrument, drove straight through the creature's body. Frigid air erupted from the cylinder until an internal emergency seal restored its atmospheric integrity.

Prone on her bed of uneasy dreams Newt moaned

softly, her head turning to one side, eyes moving beneath
closed lids. But she did not wake up. The cylinder's
integrity had been restored just in time to save her life.

Emitting periodic, unearthly shrieks the mortally wounded
crawler flung itself across the room, legs and tail flailing
spasmodically at the transparent sliver which pierced its
body. It landed atop the cylinder in which reposed the
motionless Hicks, its legs convulsively gripping the crest of
the dome. Shuddering, quivering, it clawed at the metallic
glass while acidic body fluids pumped from the wound.
They ate into the glass, into the metal base of the cylinder,
into and through the floor. Smoke began to rise from
somewhere beneath the deck, filling the chamber.

Around the room, throughout the ship, telltales winked
to life, warning lights began to flash and Klaxons to sound.
There was no one awake to hear them, but that did not affect
the *Sulaco*'s reaction. It was doing its job, complying with
its programming. Meanwhile smoke continued to billow
from the ragged aperture in the floor. Atop Hicks's cylinder
the crawler humped obscenely as it continued to bleed
destruction.

A female voice, calm and serenely artificial, echoed
unheard within the chamber. "Attention. Explosive gases
are accumulating within the cryogenic compartment. Explosive gases are accumulating within the cryogenic compartment."

Flush-mounted fans began to hum within the ceiling,
inhaling the swirling, thickening gas. Acid continued to drip
from the now motionless, dead crawler.

Beneath the floor something exploded. Bright, actin-
ic light flared, to be followed by a spurt of sharp yellow
flame. Darker smoke began to mix with the thinner gases

that now filled the chamber. The overhead lights flickered uncertainly.

The exhaust fans stopped.

"Fire in cryogenic compartment," the unperturbed female voice declared in the tone of something with nothing to lose. "Fire in cryogenic compartment."

A nozzle emerged from the ceiling, rotating like a miniature cannon. It halted, focusing on the flames and gas emerging from the hole in the floor. Liquid bubbled at its tip, gushed in the direction of the blaze. For an instant the flames were subdued.

Sparks erupted from the base of the nozzle. The burgeoning stream died, dribbling ineffectively from the powerhead.

"Fire suppression system inactivated. Fire suppression system inactivated. Exhaust system inactivated. Exhaust system inactivated. Fire and explosive gases in cryogenic chamber."

Motors hummed to life. The four functioning cryonic cylinders rose from their cradles on hydraulic supports. Their telltales winking, they began to move to the far side of the room. Some and intensifying flame obscured but did not slow their passage. Still pierced through by the chunk of metallic glass, the dead crawler slid off the moving coffin and fell to the floor.

"All personnel report to EEV," the voice insisted, its tone unchanged. "Precautionary evacuation in one minute."

Moving in single file the cryonic cylinders entered a transport tube, traveled at high speed trough the bowels of the ship until they emerged in the starboard lock, there to be loaded by automatic handlers into the waiting Emergency

Escape Vehicle. They were its only occupants. Behind the transparent faceplate, Newt twitched in her sleep.

Lights flashed, motors hummed. The voice spoke even though there were none to hear. "All EEVs will be jettisoned in ten seconds. Nine. . . ."

Interior locks slammed shut, externals opened wide. The voice continued its countdown.

At "zero" two things happened with inimical simultaneity: ten EEVs, nine of them empty, were ejected from the ship, and the proportion of escaping gases within the damaged cryogenic chamber interacted critically with the flames that were emerging from the acid-leached hole in the floor. For a brief eruptive instant the entire fore port side of the *Sulaco* blazed in fiery imitation of the distant stars.

Half the fleeing EEVs were severely jolted by the explosion. Two began tumbling, completely out of control. One embarked upon a short, curving path which brought it back in a wide, sweeping arc to the ship from which it had been ejected. It did not slow as it neared its storage pod. Instead it slammed at full acceleration into the side of the transport. A second, larger explosion rocked the great vessel. Wounded, it lurched onward through emptiness, periodically emitting irregular bursts of light and heat while littering the immaculate void with molten, shredded sections of its irrevocably damaged self.

On board the escape craft containing the four cryonic cylinders, telltales were flashing, circuits flickering and sparking. The EEV's smaller, less sophisticated computers struggled to isolate, minimize, and contain the damage that had been caused by the last-second explosion. The vehicle had not been hulled, but the concussion had damaged sensitive instrumentation.

It sought status clarification from the mother ship and when none was forthcoming, instigated a scan of its immediate surroundings. Halfway through the hasty survey the requisite instrumentation failed but it was quickly rejuvenated via a backup system. The *Sulaco* had been journeying far off the beaten photonic path, its mission having carried it to the fringes of human exploration. It had not traveled long upon its homeward path when overcome by disaster. Mankind's presence in this section of space was marked but intermittent, his installations far apart and few between.

The EEV's guiding computer found something. Undesirable, not a primary choice. But under existing conditions it was the only choice. The ship could not estimate how long it could continue to function given the serious nature of the damage it had suffered. Its primary task was the preservation of the human life it bore. A course was chosen and set. Still sputtering, striving mightily to repair itself, the compact vessel's drive throbbed to life.

Fiorina wasn't an impressive world, and in appearance even less inviting, but it was the only one in the Neroid Sector with an active beacon. The EEV's data banks locked in on the steady signal. Twice the damaged navigation system lost the beam, but continued on the prescribed course anyway. Twice the signal was recovered. Information on Fiorina was scarce and dated, as befitted its isolation and peculiar status.

"Fiorina 'Fury' 361," the readout stated. "Outer veil mineral ore refinery. Maximum security work-correctional facility." The words meant nothing to the ship's computer. They would have meant much to its passengers, but they were not in position or condition to read anything. "Additional information requested?" the computer flashed plaintively.

When the proper button was not immediately pressed, the screen obediently blanked.

Days later the EEV plunged toward the gray, roiling atmosphere of its destination. There was nothing inviting about the dark clouds that obscured the planetary surface. No glimpse of blue or green showed through them, no indication of life. But the catalog indicated the presence of a human installation, and the communications beacon threw its unvarying pulse into emptiness with becoming steadiness.

On-board systems continued to fail with discouraging regularity. The EEV's computer strained to keep the craft under control as one backup after another kicked in. Clouds the color of coal dust raced past the unoccupied ports as atmospheric lightning flashed threateningly off the chilled, sealed coffins within.

The computer experienced no strain as it tried to bring the EEV down safely. There was no extra urgency in its efforts. It would have functioned identically had the sky been clear and the winds gentle, had its own internal systems been functioning optimally instead of flaring and failing with progressive regularity.

The craft's landing gear had not responded to the drop command and there was neither time nor power to try a second approach. Given the jumbled, precipitous nature of the landscape immediately surrounding the beacon and formal landing site, the computer opted to try for a touchdown on the relatively smooth sand beach.

When additional power was requested, it developed that it did not exist. The computer tried. That was its job. But the EEV fell far short of the beach, slamming into the sea at too acute an angle.

Within the compartment, braces and bulkheads struggled to absorb the impact. Metal and carbon composites groaned, buffeted by forces they were never intended to withstand. Support struts cracked or bent, walls twisted. The computer concentrated all its efforts on trying to ensure that the four cylinders in its care remained intact. The crisis left little time for much else. About itself the computer cared nothing. Self-care was not a function with which it had been equipped. The surface of Fiorina was as barren as its sky, a riot of gray-black stone scoured by howling winds. A few twisted, contorted growths clung to protected hollows in the rock. Driving rain agitated the surface of dank, cold pools.

The inanimate shapes of heavy machinery dotted the mournful landscape. Loaders, transports, and immense excavators and lifters rested where they had been abandoned, too massive and expensive to evacuate from the incredibly rich site which had once demanded their presence. Three immense burrowing excavators sat facing the wind like a trio of gigantic carnivorous worms, their drilling snouts quiescent, their operator compartments dark and deserted. Smaller machines and vehicles clustered in groups like so many starving parasites, as if waiting for one of the larger machines to grind to life so they might eagerly gather crumbs from its flanks.

Below the site dark breakers smashed methodically into a beach of gleaming black sand, expending their energy on a lifeless shore. No elegant arthropods skittered across the surface of that shadowy bay, no birds darted down on skilled, questing wings to probe the broken edges of the incoming waves for small, edible things.

There were fish in the waters, though. Strange, elongated creatures with bulging eyes and small, sharp teeth. The human transients who called Fiorina home engaged in occasional arguments as to their true nature, but as these people were not the sort for whom a lengthy discussion of the nature of parallel evolution was the preferred mode of entertainment, they tended to accept the fact that the ocean-going creatures, whatever their peculiar taxonomy, were edible, and let it go at that. Fresh victuals of any kind were scarce. Better perhaps not to peer too deeply into the origins of whatever ended up in the cookpot, so long as it was palatable.

The man walking along the beach was thoughtful and in no particular hurry. His intelligent face was preoccupied, his expression noncommittal. Light plastic attire protected his perfectly bald head from the wind and rain. Occasionally he kicked in irritation at the alien insects which swarmed around his feet, seeking a way past the slick, treated plastic. While Fiorina's visitors occasionally sought to harvest the dubious bounty of its difficult waters, the more primitive native life-forms were not above trying to feast on the visitors.

He strolled silently past abandoned derricks and fossilized cranes, wholly intent on his thoughts. He did not smile. His attitude was dominated by a quiet resignation born not of determination but indifference, as though he cared little about what happened today, or whether there was a tomorrow. In any event he found far more pleasure in gazing inward. His all too familiar surroundings gave him little pleasure.

A sound caused him to look up. He blinked, wiping cold drizzle from his face mask. The distant roar drew his gaze to a point in the sky. Without warning a lowering cloud gave violent birth to a sliver of descending metal. It glowed softly and the air around it screamed as it fell.

He gazed at the place where it had struck the ocean, pausing before resuming his walk.

Halfway up the beach he checked his chronometer,

then turned and began to retrace his steps. Occasionally he glanced out to sea. Seeing nothing, he expected to find nothing. So the limp form which appeared on the sand ahead of him was a surprise. He increased his pace slightly and bent over the body as wavelets lapped around his feet. For the first time his blood began to race slightly. The body was that of a woman, and she was still alive. He rolled her over onto her back.

Stared down into Ripley's unconscious, salt-streaked face.

He looked up, but the beach still belonged to him alone. Him, and this utterly unexpected new arrival. Leaving her to go for help would mean delaying treatment which might save her life, not to mention exposing her to the small but still enthusiastic predators which inhabited parts of Fiorina.

Lifting her beneath her arms, he heaved once and managed to get her torso around his shoulders. Legs straining, he lifted. With the woman on his shoulders and back he headed slowly toward the weather lock from which he'd emerged earlier.

Inside he paused to catch his breath, then continued on toward the bug wash. Three prisoners who'd been working outside were busy delousing, naked beneath the hot, steady spray that mixed water with disinfectant. As medical officer, Clemens carried a certain amount of authority. He used it now.

"Listen up!" The men turned to regard him curiously. Clemens interacted infrequently with the prisoners except for those who sought him out for sick call. Their initial indifference vanished as soon as they spotted the body hanging from his shoulders. "An EEV's come down." They exchanged glances. "Don't just stand there," he snapped, trying to divert their attention from his burden. "Get out on the beach. There may be others. And notify Andrews."

They hesitated, then began to move. As they exited the wash and began grabbing at their clothes, they stared at the woman Clemens carried. He didn't dare set her down.

- II -

Andrews didn't like working the Communicator. Every use went down in his permanent record. Deep-space communication was expensive and he was expected to make use of the device only when absolutely and unavoidably necessary. It might develop that his judgment would not agree with that of some slick-assed bonehead back at headquarters, in which case his accumulated pay might be docked, or he might be denied a promotion. All without a chance to defend himself, because by the time he made it out of the hellhole that was Fiorina and back home, the cretin who'd docked him would probably be long since dead or retired.

Hell, why was he worrying? Everyone he'd ever known would be dead by the time he got back home. That didn't render him any less anxious to make that oft-anticipated journey.

So he did his rotten job as best he could and hoped that

his rotten employers would eventually take note of his skill and professionalism and offer early retirement, except that now a rotten, unforeseen difficulty had arisen with the sole intent of complicating his life. Andrews harbored an intense dislike for the unforeseen. One of the few compensations of his job was its unremitting predictability.

Until now. And it compelled him to make use of the Communicator. Angrily he hammered the keys.

FURY 361—CLASS C PRISON UNIT—IRIS 12037154.
REPORT EEV UNIT 2650 CRASH
OCCUPANTS - BISHOP MODEL ANDROID,
                  INACTIVE HICKS, CPL.—ES
                  MARINES—L55321—DOA RIPLEY,
                  LT.—CO SVC.——B515617—
                  SURVIVOR UNIDENTIFIED
                  JUVENILE FEMALE—DOA
REQUEST EMERG. EVAC. SOONEST POSSIBLE—
AWAIT RESPONSE SUPT. ANDREWS M51021.

[Time delay transmis 1844—Fiorina]

Clemens had dragged the woman out of the water and had hustled her up to the facility as quickly as possible. So quickly that her condition and not her gender had dominated their thoughts. Reflection would come later, and with it the problems Andrews envisioned.

As for the EEV itself, they'd used the mutated oxen to winch it ashore. Any of the mine vehicles could have done the job quicker and easier, but those which had been abandoned outside had long since given up the ghost of active function, and those within the complex were too valuable to the inhabitants to risk exposing to the weather, even assuming the men could have safely hoisted an appropriate vehicle outside. Simpler to use the oxen, unaccustomed as they were to the task. But they performed effectively, save for one that collapsed subsequently and died, doubtless from having been subjected to the unfamiliar strain of actual work.

Once within reach of the mine's sole remaining operational external crane, it was easy enough to secure the badly damaged escape craft to the bracing and lower it inside. Andrews was there when the men went in, soon to emerge and declare that the woman hadn't come alone, that there were others.

The superintendent wasn't pleased. More complications, more holes in his placid daily routine. More decisions to make. He didn't like making decisions. There was always the danger of making a wrong one.

The marine corporal was dead, likewise the unfortunate child. The android didn't matter. Andrews was somewhat relieved. Only the woman to deal with, then, and just as well. She presented complications enough.

One of the men informed him that the Communicator was holding an on-line message. Leaving the EEV and its contents in the care of others, the superintendent made his way back to his office. He was a big man in his late forties, muscular, powerful, determined. He had to be all of that and more or he'd never have been assigned to Fiorina.

The reply was as terse as his original communication.
TO: FURY 361—CLASS C PRISON UNIT 1237154
FROM: NETWORK CONCOM 01500—WEYLAND-
YUTANI MESSAGE RECEIVED.

Well, now, that was profound. Andrews stared at the readout screen but nothing else was forthcoming. No suggestions, no requests for additional information, no elegant corporate explication. No criticism, no praise. Somehow he'd expected more.

He could send another message requesting more data,

except that the powers-that-be were likely to deem it extraneous and dock his pay for the cost. They'd responded, hadn't they? Even if they hadn't exactly replied. There was nothing he could do but deal with the situation as best he saw fit . . . and wait.

Another dream. No sense of time in dreams, no temporal spaciousness. People see all sorts of things in dreams, both intensely realistic and wholly imaginary. Rarely do they see clocks.

The twin-barreled flamethrower was heavy in her hands as she cautiously approached the cryonic cylinders. A quick check revealed all three occupants untouched, undisturbed. Bishop, quiescent in fragments. Newt ethereal in her perfect childish beauty, so foreign to the place and time in which she unwillingly found herself. Hicks peaceful, unmarred. She felt herself hesitating as she drew near, but his dome remained shut, his eyes closed.

A sound and she whirled, flipping a switch on the weapon's ribs even as her finger convulsed on the trigger. The device emitted a plastic click. That was all. Frantically she tried again. A short, reluctant burst of flame emerged a few inches from one of the barrels, died.

Panicky, she inspected the weapon, checking the fill levels, the trigger, those leads that were visible. Everything seemed functional. It ought to work, it had to work. . . .

Something nearby, close. She dreamt herself retreating, backing up cautiously, seeking the protection of a solid wall as she fumbled with the flamethrower. It was near. She knew it too well to think otherwise. Her fingers wrestled with the balky device. She'd found the trouble, she was sure. A minute more, that was all she needed. Recharge this, reset, then ready to fire. Half a minute. She happened to glance downward.

The alien's tail was between her legs.

She spun screaming, right into its waiting arms, and tried to bring the flamethrower to bear. A hand clutched; horribly elegant, incredibly powerful fingers crushed the weapon in the middle, collapsing the twin barrels, the other arm trapping her. She pummeled the shiny, glistening thorax with her fists. Useless the gesture, useless everything now.

It spun her around and shoved her across the nearest cryonic pod. Shoved again. Her face was pressed tight to the cool, inorganic glass. Beneath her, Hicks opened his eyes and smiled again. And again.

She screamed.

The infirmary was compact and nearly empty. It abutted a much larger medical facility designed to handle dozens of patients a day. Those miners, prospective patients, were long gone from Fiorina. They had accomplished their task years ago, extracting the valuable ore from the ground and then following it back home. Only the prisoners remained, and they had no need of such extensive facilities.

So the larger unit had been gutted of salvageable material and the smaller semi-surgery turned over to the prison. Cheaper that way. Less room to heat, less energy required, money saved. Where prisoners were concerned that was always the best way.

Not that they'd been left with nothing. Supplies and equipment were more than ample for the installation's needs. The Company could afford to be generous. Besides, shipping even worthwhile material offworld was expensive. Better to leave some of it, the lesser quality stuff, and gain credit for concomitant compassion. The good publicity was worth more than the equipment.

Besides the facility there was Clemens. Like some of the supplies he was too good for Fiorina, though it would have been difficult to convince anyone familiar with his case of that. Nor would he have raised much in the way of objections. But the prisoners were lucky to have him, and they knew it. Most of them were not stupid. Merely unpleasant. It was a combination which in some men gave rise to captains of industry and pillars of government. In others it led merely to defeat and degradation. When this situation was directed inward the sufferers were treated or incarcerated on places like Earth.

When it erupted outward to encompass the innocent it led elsewhere. To Fiorina, for example. Clemens was only one of many who'd realized too late that his personal path diverged from the normal run of humanity to lead instead to this place.

The woman was trying to say something. Her lips were moving and she was straining upward, though whether pushing against or away from something he was unable to tell. Leaning close, he put his ear to her mouth. Sounds emergent, bubbling and gurgling, as if rising toward the surface from deep within.

He straightened and turned her head to one side, holding it firmly but gently. Gagging, choking, she vomited forth a stream of dark salt water. The heaving ended quickly and she subsided, still unconscious but resting quietly now; still, easy. He eased her head back onto the pillow, gazing solemnly at her masklike visage. Her features were delicate, almost girlish despite her age. There was about her the air of someone who had spent too much time as a tourist in hell.

Well, being dumped out of a ship via EEV and then awakened and revived from deep sleep by a crash into the sea would be enough to mark anyone, he told himself.

The infirmary door hissed softly as it slid back to admit Andrews and Aaron. Clemens wasn't crazy about either the superintendent or his number two. At the same time he was quite aware that Andrews wasn't in love with the facility's sole medical technician either. Though in status he might be a notch above the general population, Clemens was still a prisoner serving sentence, a fact neither of the two men ever let him forget. Not that he was likely to. Many things were difficult to accomplish on Fiorina, but forgetting was impossible.

They halted by the side of the bed and stared down at its motionless occupant. Andrews grunted at nothing in particular.

"What's her status, Mr. Clemens?"

The technician sat back slightly, glanced up at the man who for all practical purposes served as Fiorina's lord and master.

"She's alive."

Andrews's expression tightened and he favored the tech with a sardonic smile. "Thank you, Mr. Clemens. That's very helpful. And while I suppose I wouldn't, or shouldn't, want it to be otherwise, it also does mean that we have a problem, doesn't it?"

"Not to worry, sir. I think we can pull her through. There's no internal bleeding, nothing broken, not even a serious sprain. I think she'll make a complete recovery."

"Which, as you know, Mr. Clemens, is precisely what concerns me." He stared appraisingly at the woman in the bed. "I wish she hadn't come here. I wish she wasn't here now."

"Without wishing to sound disrespectful, sir, I have this feeling that she'd eagerly concur with you. Based on what I was told about her landing and having seen for myself the current condition of her EEV, I'm of the opinion that she didn't have a whole hell of a lot of choice in the matter. Any idea where they're from? What ship?"

"No," Andrews muttered. "I Notified Weyland-Y."

"They answer?" Clemens was holding Ripley's wrist, ostensibly to check her pulse.

"if you can call it that. They acknowledged receipt of my message. That's all. Guess they're not feeling real talkative."

"Understandable, if they had an interest in the ship that was lost. Probably running around like mad trying to decide what your report signifies." The mental image of confounded Company nabobs pleased him.

"Let me know if there's any change in her condition."

"Like if she should conveniently expire?"

Andrews glared at him. "I'm already upset enough over this as it is, Clemens. Be smart. Don't make it worse. And don't make me start thinking of it and you in the same breath. There's no need for excessive morbidity. It may surprise you to learn that I hope she lives. Though if she regains consciousness she may think otherwise. Let's go," he told his factotum. The two men departed.

The woman moaned softly, her head shifting nervously from side to side. Physical reaction, Clemens wondered, or side effects of the medication he'd hastily and hopefully dumped into her system? He sat watching her, endlessly grateful for the opportunity to relax in her orbit, for the chance simply to be close to her, study her, smell her. He'd all but forgotten what it was like to be in a woman's presence. The memories returned rapidly, jolted by her appearance. Beneath the bruises and strain she was quite beautiful, he thought. More, much more, than he'd had any right to expect.

She moaned again. Not the medication, he decided, or pain from her injuries. She was dreaming. No harm there. After all, a few dreams couldn't hurt her.

The dimly lit assembly hall was four stories high. Men hung from the second floor railing, murmuring softly to each other, some smoking various combinations of plant and chemical. The upper levels were deserted. Like most of the Fiorina mine, it was designed to accommodate far more than the couple of dozen men presently gathered together in its cavernous depths.

They had assembled at the superintendent's request. All twenty-five of them. Hard, lean, bald, young and not so young, and those for whom youth was but a fading warm memory. Andrews sat confronting them, his second-in-command Aaron nearby. Clemens stood some distance away from both prisoners and jailers, as befitted his peculiar status.

Two jailers, twenty-five prisoners. They could have jumped the superintendent and his assistant at any time, overpowered them with comparative ease. To what end? Revolt would only give them control of the installation they already ran. There was nowhere to escape to, no better place on Fiorina that they were forbidden to visit. When the next supply ship arrived and ascertained the situation, it would simply decline to drop supplies and would file a report. Heavily armed troops would follow, the revolutionaries would be dealt with, and all who had participated and survived would find their sentences extended.

The small pleasures that might be gained from defiance of authority were not worth another month on Fiorina, much less another year or two. The most obdurate prisoners realized as much. So there were no revolts, no challenges to Andrews's authority. Survival on and, more importantly, escape from Fiorina depended on doing what was expected of one. The prisoners might not be content, but they were pacific.

Aaron surveyed the murmuring crowd, raised his voice impatiently. "All right, all right. Let's pull it together, get it going. Right? Right. If you please, Mr. Dillon."

Dillon stepped forward. He was a leader among the imprisoned and not merely because of his size and strength. The wire rimless glasses he wore were far more an affectation, a concession to tradition, than a necessity. He preferred them to contacts, and of course the Company could hardly be expected to expend time and money to provide a prisoner with transplants. That suited Dillon fine. The glasses were antiques, a family heirloom which had somehow survived the generations intact. They served his requirements adequately.

The single dreadlock that hung from his otherwise naked pate swung slowly as he walked. It took a lot of time and effort to keep the hirsute decoration free of Fiorina's persistent bugs, but he tolerated the limited discomfort in order to maintain the small statement of individuality.

He cleared his throat distinctly. "Give us strength, Oh Lord, to endure. We recognize that we are poor sinners in the hands of an angry God. Let the circle be unbroken...until the day. Amen." It was a brief invocation. It was enough. Upon its conclusion the body of prisoners raised their right fists, lowered them silently. The gesture was one of acceptance and resignation, not defiance. On Fiorina defiance bought you nothing except the ostracism of your companions and possibly an early grave.

Because if you got too far out of line Andrews could and would exile you from the installation, with comparative impunity. There was no one around to object, to check on him, to evaluate the correctness of his actions. No independent board of inquiry to follow up a prisoner's death. Andrews proposed, Andrews imposed. It would have been intolerable save for the fact that while the superintendent was a hard man, he was also fair. The prisoners considered themselves fortunate at that. It could easily have been otherwise.

He surveyed his charges. He knew each of them intimately, far better than he would have liked to, had he been given the option. He knew their individual strengths and weaknesses, distastes and peccadilloes, the details of their case histories. Some of them were scum, others merely fatally antisocial, and there was a broad range in between. He cleared his throat importantly.

"Thank you, gentlemen. There's been a lot of talk about what happened early this morning, most of it frivolous. So you can consider this a rumor control session.

"Here are the facts. As some of you know, a 337 model EEV crash-landed here at 0600 on the morning watch. There was one survivor, two dead, and a droid that was smashed beyond hope of repair." He paused briefly to let that sink in.

"The survivor is a woman."

The mumbling began. Andrews listened, watched intently, trying to note the extent of reactions. It wasn't bad . . . yet.

One of the prisoners leaned over the upper railing. Morse was in his late twenties but looked older. Fiorina aged its unwilling citizens quickly. He sported a large number of gold-anodized teeth, a consequence of certain antisocial activities. The gold color was a cosmetic choice. He seemed jumpy, his normal condition.

"I just want to say that when I arrived here I took a vow of celibacy. That means no women. No sex of any kind." His agitated stare swept the assembly. "We all took the vow. Now, let me say that I, for one, do not appreciate Company policy allowing her to freely intermingle . . ."

As he droned on, Aaron whispered to his superior. "Cheeky bastard, ain't he, sir?"

Finally Dillon stepped in front of his fellow prisoner, his resonant voice soft but firm. "What brother means to say is that we view the presence of any outsider, especially a woman, as a violation of the harmony, a potential break of the spiritual unity that gets us through each day and keeps us sane. You hear what I say, Superintendent? You take my meaning?"

Andrews met Dillon's gaze unflinchingly. "Believe me, we are well aware of your feelings in this matter. I assure you, all of you, that everything will be done to accommodate your concerns and that this business will be rectified as soon as possible. I think that's in everyone's best interest." Murmurs rose from the crowd.

"You will be pleased to know that I have already requested a rescue team. Hopefully, they will be here inside of a week to evacuate her ASAP." Someone in the middle spoke up. "A week, Superintendent? Nobody can get here that fast. Not from anywhere."

Andrews eyed the man. "Apparently there's a ship in transit to Motinea. She's been in the program for months. This is an emergency. There are rules even the Company has to comply with. I'm sure they'll contact her, kick at least a pilot out of deep sleep, and divert her our way to make the pickup. And that will put an end to that."

He knew no such thing, of course, but it was the logical course of action for the Company to take and he felt a certain confidence in presupposing. If the ship bound for Motinea didn't divert, then he'd deal with the situation as required. One potential crisis at a time.

He glanced up at Clemens. "Have you had enough time to make an evaluation?"

The tech crossed his arms diffidently across his chest. "Sort of. Best I can manage, with what we have here."

"Never mind the complaints. What's her medical status?"

Clemens was well aware that every eye in the room was suddenly focused on him, but he didn't acknowledge them, keeping his attention on the superintendent. "She doesn't seem too badly damaged. Mostly just bruised and banged up. One of her ribs may be broken. If so it's only a stress fracture. What is potentially more dangerous is that she came out of deep sleep too abruptly." He paused to collect his thoughts.

"Look, I'm just a general tech and even I can see that she's going to need specialist attention. Somebody gets whacked out of deep sleep early, without the appropriate biophysical prep, and there can be all kinds of problems. Unpredictable side effects, latent respiratory and circulatory complications, cellular disruptions that sometimes don't manifest themselves for days or weeks—stuff I wouldn't begin to know how to diagnose, much less properly treat. For her sake I hope that rescue ship carries full medical facilities."

"Will she live?" Andrews asked him.

The tech shook his head in quiet wonder. The superintendent was good at hearing only what he wanted to hear.

"Assuming nothing shows up later, I think she'll be fine. But don't quote me on that. Especially to a registered physician."

"What're you afraid of?" Someone sniggered behind him. "Bein' accused of malpractice?" Inclement laughter rose from some in the group.

Andrews stepped on it quickly, before Clemens or anyone else could reply. "Look, none of us here is naive. It's in everybody's best interests if the woman doesn't come out of the infirmary until the rescue team arrives. And certainly not without an escort. Out of sight, out of mind, right?" No one chose to comment one way or the other. "So we should all stick to our set routines and not get unduly agitated. Correct? All right." He rose. "Thank you, gentlemen."

No one moved. Dillon turned and spoke softly. "Okay."

The assemblage began to break up, the men to return to their daily tasks. Andrews was not miffed by the slight. It was a small gesture by the prisoners, and he was willing to allow small gestures. It let some of the pressure off, mitigated their need to attempt big ones.

The meeting had gone as well as could have been expected. He felt he'd dealt with the situation properly, putting a stop to rumor and speculation before it could get out of hand. Aaron at his side, he headed back to his office.

A more informative response from the Company would have been helpful, however.

Clemens found his exit blocked by Dillon. "Something on your mind?"

The big man looked concerned. "Pill pusher. You should be careful of this woman."

Clemens smiled. "She's not in any condition to cause much trouble. Don't we owe all God's children a fighting chance?"

"We don't know whose child she is." The two men stared at each other a moment longer. Then Dillon moved aside to let the tech pass. His gaze followed Clemens until he stepped through the portal leading to tunnel D.

The woman lay motionless on the bed, for a change not moaning, not dreaming. Clemens checked the IV pack taped to her arm. Without knowing the specifics of her condition he'd been forced to treat her for general debilitation. In addition to glucose and sucrose the pack contained a broad range of tolerant antibiotics in solution, REM-sleep modifiers, and painkillers. The tough ID tag she'd been wearing had been damaged in the crash, so he'd been forced to treat her without the crucial information it contained. He'd monitored her carefully for any signs of rejection and was relieved when none manifested themselves. At least she wasn't allergic to anything he'd pumped into her system so far.

He was gratified to see that the armpack was nearly empty. That meant her body was making good use of the rehab solution. The readouts on the VS checker as he passed it over her chest and skull stayed green. Thus encouraged, he slipped a capsule into the injector and turned her arm slightly to expose more of the tricep.

Her eyes snapped open as if she'd only been faking sleep. Startled by the speed of her reaction, he hesitated. She indicated the device in his hand.

"What's that?"

"General site injector."

"I can see that. You know what I mean."

He smiled slightly. "A light cocktail of my own devising. Sort of an eye-opener. Adrenaline, some selected designer endorphins, a couple of mystery proteins. For flavor. I think your body's recovered sufficiently to metabolize them. Five minutes after they've dispersed through your system you'll feel a lot better than you do now."

She continued to eye him warily. "Are you a doctor?"

He shrugged and looked away momentarily, as if the question made him uncomfortable. "General med tech. I've only got a 3-C rating. But I'm the best you're going to find around here." He leaned forward, eyes narrowing as he inspected her hair appraisingly. "I really ought to shave your head. Should've done it right away but I was busy with more important things."

This admission caused Ripley to sit bolt upright in the bed, clutching the sheet protectively to her neck.

"Take it easy. I'm no murderer. Though you'll find them here."

"Why do you have to shave my head?"

"Microscopic parasites. Carnivorous arthropods. They're endemic to Fiorina. Fortunately they don't find humans particularly tasty... except for the keratin in our hair. For some reason they don't have the same appetite for finger-nails. Wrong consistency, maybe. We just call 'em lice, and to hell with scientific nomenclature."

"Can't you use some kind of spray, or prophylactic shampoo, something?" Her eyes remained fixed on the razor.

"Oh, the Company tried that when they were starting up the mine, but these little suckers are tough. Anything'd have to be to make a success of it on this world. Turned out that anything strong enough to dent the parasites raised blisters on the skin. Bad enough on the scalp. Damn sight worse lower down. Shaving turned out to be a simpler, cheaper, and more effective solution. Some of the guys hang on to a little hair out of spite and fight the bugs as best they can. Eyebrows, for example. You wouldn't think anybody would give a damn about something as ephemeral as eye-brows. But dense hair, that's out of the question. Try to live with the lice and they'll drive you crazy, crawling around, eating, itching—"

"All right, all right," Ripley replied quickly. "I get the picture."

"I'll give you an electric razor for downstairs. When you're feeling better you can attend to that. The infirmary's about the most sterile room in the installation, so you should be okay for a while, but the little buggers'll find you eventually. They're too small to screen out. Just shave and they won't bother you." She hesitated, thoughtful, then nodded understandingly.

"My name is Clemens. I'm the chief medical officer here at Fury 361."

Her brows knitted. "That doesn't sound like a mine designation."

"Mine's what it used to be. Last of the worthwhile ore was dug out, refined, and shipped offworld some time ago. Weyland-Yutani had this huge facility cost that forced them to abandon, so to recoup a few credits they lease the operative part of it for a maximum-security prison. Everybody benefits. Society is separated from its most undesirable undesirables and the Company gets free caretakers. Everybody benefits, except those of us who are sent here." He gestured with the injector. "Do you mind? This is just sort of a stabilizer."

She was feeling safe enough now to let him approach as she turned her attention to examining her surroundings. "How did I get here?"

"You crash-landed in an EEV. Nobody knows what happened to your mothership or what caused you to be ejected. If Harry Andrews—he's the superintendent here—knows, he isn't saying.

"Whatever catastrophe caused you to be ejected also

must have damaged the landing controls on the EEV because you smacked into the bay pretty hard. We hauled it back here. I haven't been inside myself, but if the exterior's any indication of the kind of internal damage she suffered, you're damn lucky to be alive, much less more or less in one piece.''

She swallowed. ''What about the others?''

''Yeah, I was kind of wondering about that myself. Where's the rest of the crew? did they get off on other EEVs?''

''There is no 'rest of the crew,' '' she informed him tersely. ''It's a long story, one I don't feel much like telling right now. I mean what about those who were in the EEV with me? How many were there?''

''Two. Three if you count the android.'' He paused. ''I'm afraid they didn't make it.''

''What?'' It wasn't sinking in.

''They didn't survive.''

She considered for a long moment, then shook her head brusquely. ''I want to go to the ship. I have to see for myself.'' She started to sit up and he put a restraining hand on her shoulder.

''Hey, hang on. As your doctor, I have to tell you that you're in no condition for that.''

''You're not a doctor, remember?'' She slipped out of the other side of the bed and stood waiting expectantly, quite naked. ''You want to get me some clothes, or should I go like this?

Clemens took his time deciding, not entirely displeased by the opportunity to view her vertically. ''Given the nature of our indigenous population, I would strongly suggest clothes.'' Rising, he opened a locker on the far side of the infirmary and began sorting through the contents.

"Keep in mind as you gambol through our little wonderland that the prison population here is strictly male and none of them have seen a woman in years. Neither have I, for that matter."

She waited, hand on hip, giving him the calculating eye. "Yeah, but I don't have to worry about you, because you're a not-doctor, remember?"

He grinned in spite of himself.

Clemens noted how her eyes darted to and fro as he led her through the corridors and along the walkways. Like those of a nervous child . . . or sophisticated predator. She missed nothing. The slightest sound drew her instant attention. Their feet made little noise on the worn metal. The garb he'd scavenged for her was a little small, but she didn't seem to mind.

"I've no idea how long you were in deep sleep, but coming out of it the way you did can be a helluva jolt to the system. Just so you don't panic if I look at you crossways, you should know that I'm still monitoring you for possible delayed side effects. So let's steady on as we go, Ripley."

She looked at him sharply. "How do you know my name?"

"It's stenciled on the back of your shorts." He smiled apologetically. "We also found your ID tag. It was so mangled the computer could hardly read it, but we got that much off it. Unfortunately, most of your personal medical info was scrambled. I had to guess a lot.''

Ripley rolled her shoulders forward experimentally, let her head roll from side to side. "Feels like you did a pretty good job. Thanks.''

To his immense surprise he found that he was slightly embarrassed. "Hey, any jerk can slap on an armpack.''

She grinned. "I don't think so. It takes a specially qualified jerk.''

The work crew was being as careful as possible with the hulk of the EEV as they eased it onto hastily raised blocks. The old crane groaned with the effort. There hadn't been much call for its use since the mine had been shut down, and temporary reactivation for the purpose of manipulating the emergency vehicle had been a touchy process. But the machinery was responding adequately. Cables sang as the craft was gently lowered.

It had attracted its share of stares when it had first been hauled inside the complex. Ripley drew rather more as she and Clemens approached. She did a much better job of pretending not to notice than the prisoners did of trying not to look.

"Just what kind of place is this work prison?'' she asked her guide as they started up a ramp toward the battered lifeship.

Clemens stayed close. "Used to be a mine cum refinery. Mostly platinum-group minerals. Naturally the raw ore was refined on the spot. Much cheaper than shipping it offworld for processing elsewhere. I understand there was a considerable rise in the price of platinum about the time the ore body here was located. Otherwise it wouldn't have been worth the Company's while to go to the expense of setting up a facility this size this far from any point of consumption. It was a rich lode, highly concentrated.''

"And now?" She had stopped outside the EEV and was inspecting the damaged hull.

"Weyland-Yutani's got it on hold. Interstellar commodities trading isn't exactly my specialty and I don't know that anybody here gets their jollies from following the relevant rises and falls in raw materials prices. I think I heard that a drop in the price of the refined metal was accompanied by less need for the stuff.

"So most of the equipment here's been mothballed. Not worth the expense of moving it, not worth enough as salvage. There's still ore in the ground and if the price goes up I'm sure the Company would reopen. That means we'd probably get moved. Wouldn't do to have felons associating with nice, moral miners. Not that anybody would mind being shifted off this rock. The change would be sweet and it's pretty hard to conceive of anyplace else being worse.

"So we're just caretakers, just a custodial staff. Keeps things from freezing up in case the price of the ore or the need for it goes back up. Works out well for the government and the Company."

"I'd think you'd go crazy after a year or so in a place like this."

Clemens had to laugh. "That's what they said some of us were before we were sent here. But I don't think we are, at least not the majority of us. The isolation isn't nearly so trying if you can learn to think of yourself as a contemplative penitent instead of an incarcerated felon."

"Any women ever been here?"

"Sorry, Lieutenant Ripley. This is a double Y chromosome facility. Strictly male."

She nodded, then turned and bent to crawl through what remained of the battered air lock. Clemens let her forge a path, then followed.

The battered exterior of the craft was pristine compared to what she encountered inside. Walls were crumpled and bent, readouts and consoles smashed, equipment strewn haphazardly across the deck. The thick smell of salt water permeated everything. She paused, astonished that anything or anyone could have survived intact, much less her own fragile form.

"Where are the bodies?"

Clemens was equally taken with the extent of the destruction, marveling that Ripley had suffered no more damage than she had.

"We have a morgue. Mining's the kind of enterprise that demands one. We've put your friends in there until the investigative team arrives, probably in a week's time."

"There was an android. . . ."

Clemens made a face. "Disconnected and discombobulated. There were pieces of him all over the place. What's left was thrown in the trash. The corporal was impaled by a support beam straight through the chest. Even if he'd been conscious he'd never have known what hit him. As it was he probably never came out of deep sleep long enough to hurt."

"The girl?" She was holding a lot in, Clemens saw. He had no idea how much.

"She drowned in her cryotube. I don't imagine she was conscious when it happened. If anything, she went out more quietly than the corporal. I'm sorry."

Ripley digested this quietly. Then her shoulders began to shake and the tears came. That was all. No yelling, no screaming, no violent railing at an unfair, uncaring universe. Little Newt. Newt, who'd never had a chance. At least she was free. Wiping at her eyes, Ripley turned to survey the remains of the little girl's cryotube. The faceplate was broken, which was understandable.

Abruptly she frowned. The metal below the faceplate was strangely discolored. She leaned forward and ran her fingers over the stain.

Clemens looked on curiously. "What is it?"

Ripley rose, the emotion of the moment transformed into something else. There was no concern in her voice now, none of the tenderness he'd noted previously.

"Where is she?"

"I told you, the morgue. Don't you remember?" He eyed her with concern, worried that she might be having a reaction to something from the armpack. "You're disoriented. Half your system still thinks it's in deep sleep."

She whirled on him so suddenly that he started. "I want to see what's left of her body."

"What do you mean, what's left? The body's intact."

"Is it? I want to see it. I need to see for myself."

He frowned but held off questioning her. There was something in her expression. . . .One thing was clear: there would be no denying her access. Not that there was any reason to. He had the feeling her desire to view the corpse had nothing to do with nostalgia. Difficult on short acquaintance to figure what she was really like, but excessively morbid she wasn't.

The circular stairwell was narrow and slippery, but cut time off the long hike from the storage chamber where the EEV had been secured. Clemens was unable to contain his curiosity any longer.

"Any particular reason you're so insistent?"

"I have to make sure how she died," she replied evenly. "That is wasn't something else."

"Something else?" Under different circumstances Clemens might have been insulted. "I hate to be repetitious about a sensitive subject, but it's quite clear that her cylinder was breached and that she drowned." He considered. "Was she your daughter?"

"No," Ripley replied evenly, "she wasn't my daughter. My daughter died a long time ago."

As she spoke her eyes avoided his. But of course she was still weak and had to concentrate on the narrow, spiraling steps.

"Then why this need?"

Instead of answering directly she said, "Even though we weren't related, she was very close to me. You think I *want* to see her the way you've described her? I'd much rather remember her as she was. I wouldn't ask to do this if it wasn't damned important to me."

He started to reply, then stopped himself. Already he knew that Ripley wasn't the sort of person you could force a reply from. If she was going to tell him anything it would come in her own good time.

He unlocked the entrance and preceded her inside. A bottom drawer responded to his official key code and slid open on silent rollers. She moved up to stand alongside him and together they gazed down at the peaceful, tiny body.

"Give me a moment. Please."

Clemens nodded and walked across the room to fiddle with a readout. Occasionally he turned to watch as his companion examined the little girl's corpse. Despite the emotions that had to be tearing through her, she was efficient and thorough. When he thought a decent amount of time had passed, he rejoined her.

"Okay?" He expected a nod, perhaps a last sigh. He most definitely did not expect what she finally said.

"No. We need an autopsy."

"You're joking." He gaped at her.

"No way. You think I'd joke about something like this? We have to make sure how she died." Ripley's eyes were steel-hard.

"I told you: she drowned." He started to slide the body drawer back, only to have her intervene.

"I'm not so sure." She took a deep breath. "I want you to cut her open."

He stared at her in disbelief. "Listen to me. I think you're disoriented. Half your system's still in cryosleep."

"Look," she said in a thoroughly no-nonsense tone, "I have a very good reason for asking this and I want you to do it."

"Would you care to share this reason?" He was very composed.

She hesitated. "Isn't it enough that I'm asking?"

"No, it is not. 'Request of close personal friend' won't cut it with Company inspectors. You've got to do better than that." He stood waiting, impatient.

"All right," she said finally. "Risk of possible contagion."

"What kind of 'contagion'?" he snapped.

She was clearly reaching. "I'm not the doctor. You are."

He shook his head. "You'll have to do better than that."

"Cholera." She eyed him squarely. Her determination was remarkable.

"You can't be serious. There hasn't been a case reported in two hundred years. C'mon, tell me another. Never turn down a good laugh in this place. Smallpox, maybe? Dengue fever?"

"I am telling you. Cholera. I was part of the combat team that nuked Archeron. They were experimenting with all kinds of mutated bacterial and viral strains in what was supposed to be a safe, closed environment. Maybe you know about some of the Company's interests. The infection got loose and . . . spread. It was particularly virulent and there was no effective antidote. Nor could the infection be contained, though the people there tried."

"So they nuked the place? Seems like a pretty extreme prescription. Of course, we don't hear much out here, but it seems to me we would have heard about that."

"Really? I guess you don't work for the same Company I do. Or maybe you did hear. Your superintendent doesn't strike me as an especially loquacious kind of guy. He may know all about it and just decided there was no reason to pass the information along."

"Yeah." She had him confused, Clemens had to confess. And curious. Was Andrews hiding that particular piece of news? It wasn't as if he was obligated to keep the prisoners conversant with current events.

But cholera? Mutated strain or not, it still seemed like a pretty thin story. Of course, if she was telling the truth and the little girl's corpse was infected with something they might not be able to combat . . .

Or maybe it was a half-truth. Maybe there was a risk of some kind of infection and the cholera story was the only cover she'd been able to think up on short notice. Obviously she thought she had her reasons. She *was* military. What the hell did he know about it?

She was standing silently, watching him, waiting.

What the hell, he thought.

"As you wish."

Compared to the morgue the rest of the petrified, neglected complex was as bright and cheerful as an alpine meadow at high spring. Stainless steel cabinets lined one wall, bar codes taped to several. The tough laminated tile floor was chipped and cracked. Easy enough to repair, except that they didn't have the equipment or the necessary skills, and nobody cared anyway.

The gleaming cream-white table in the center of the room was bare beneath the overhead lights. A masked and gowned Clemens bent over the prepped corpse of the little girl and commenced the initial incision with the scalpel, pausing to wipe at his brow. It had been a long time since he'd done anything like this and not only was he badly out of practice, he wasn't at all sure why he was doing it now.

A saw sliced silently and efficiently through the under-sized rib cage.

"You're sure you want to go through with this?" he asked the staring Ripley. She ignored him, watching silently, her heart cold, emotions stored safely away where they wouldn't interfere. He shrugged and continued with the incision.

Placing both gloved hands in the opening he'd made, knuckles against knuckles, he took a deep breath and pulled apart, prying open and exposing the chest cavity. Concentrating, he peered inward, occasionally bending close and looking sideways for a different view. Eventually he straightened and relaxed his fingers.

"We have nothing unusual. Everything's where it's supposed to be. Nothing missing. No sign of disease, no unusual discoloration, no sign of contagion. I paid particular attention to the lungs. If anything, they appear abnormally healthy. Flooded with fluid, as I suspected. I'm sure analysis will show Fiorinian sea water. Kind of an odd physical state for cholera, hmmm?''

He made a final cross-lateral cut, inspected within, then glanced up. ''Still nothing. Satisfied?''

She turned away.

''Now, since I'm not entirely stupid, do you want to tell me what you're really looking for?''

Before she could reply, the far door was thrown open. The two somber figures who entered ignored it as it smashed into the interior wall.

Andrews's expression was even less convivial than usual.

''Mr. Clemens.''

''Superintendent.'' Clemens's reply was correct but not deferential. Ripley observed the unspoken byplay between the two with interest. ''I don't believe you've met Lieutenant Ripley.''

She suspected that the burly super's appraising glance lasted rather longer than he intended. His attention shifted to the operating table, then back to his med tech.

''What's going on here, Mr. Clemens?''

''Yeah, right sir,'' Aaron chipped in, a verbal as well as physical echo of his boss. ''What's going on, Mr. Clemens?''

''First, Lieutenant Ripley is feeling much better, I'm happy to say. As you can see, physically she's doing quite well.'' Andrews didn't rise to the bait. Mildly disappointed, Clemens continued. ''Second, in the interests of public health and security, I'm conducting an autopsy on the deceased child.''

"Without my authority?" The superintendent all but growled.

The tech replied matter-of-factly, not at all intimidated. "There didn't seem to be time."

Andrews's brows lifted slightly. "Don't give me that, Clemens. That's one thing we have in surplus on Fiorina."

"What I mean is that the lieutenant was concerned about the possible presence in the body of a mutated infectious organism."

The superintendent glanced questioningly at the silent Ripley. "Is that true?"

She nodded, offering no further explanation.

"It's turned out all right," Clemens interjected. "The body is perfectly normal and shows no signs of contagion. I was certain," he finished dryly, "that you'd want me to follow up on this as promptly as possible. Hence my desire to begin immediately."

You could almost see the thoughts dancing in Andrews's brain, Ripley thought. Fermenting.

"All right," he said finally, "but it might be helpful if Lieutenant Ripley didn't parade around in front of the prisoners, as I am told she did in the last hour. Semi-monastic vows notwithstanding. Nothing personal, you understand, Lieutenant. The suggestion is made as much for your protection as for my peace of mind."

"I quite understand," she murmured, half smiling.

"I'm sure that you do." He turned back to the med tech. "It might also be helpful if you kept me informed as to any change in her physical status. I'm expected to keep the official log updated on this sort of thing. Or would that be asking too much?"

Ripley took a step forward. "We have to cremate the bodies."

Andrews frowned at her. "Nonsense. We'll keep the bodies on ice until a rescue team arrives. There are forms that will need to be filled out. I don't have that kind of jurisdictional leeway."

"Cremate . . . that's a good one, sir," Aaron sniggered, always eager to please.

"Look, I'm not making an arbitrary request here," Ripley told him, "and it has nothing to do with . . . personal feelings. There is a public health issue at stake." She eyed Clemens expectantly.

What on earth is troubling her so? he found himself wondering. Aloud he said, "Lieutenant Ripley feels that the possibility of a communicable infection still exists."

The superintendent's gaze narrowed suspiciously. "I thought you said there was no sign of disease."

"What I said was that as far as I was concerned the body was clean and showed no sign of contagion. You know how sophisticated the facilities I have at my disposal are, and what an outstanding reputation I maintain in the interworld medical profession." Andrews grunted understandingly.

"Just because I pronounce the body clean doesn't mean that it necessarily is. It would appear that the child drowned plain and simple, though without the proper forensics tests it's impossible to be absolutely certain. At the risk of contradicting my own analysis I think it would be unwise to tolerate even the possibility of a mutated virus getting loose within the installation. I don't think the members of the rescue team would look kindly on such a development upon their arrival, either. It might make them rather standoffish, and we do treasure our occasional visits, don't we?

"Not to mention which a preventable outbreak of something the marines had to nuke Archeron to destroy would look very bad on your report, wouldn't it? Assuming you were still alive to care."

Andrews now looked distinctly unhappy. "Freezing the body should take care of any viruses present."

"Not necessarily," Ripley told him.

"How do you know it wouldn't?"

"We're talking complex bioengineered mutations here. How do you know that it would?"

The superintendent cursed under his breath, his troubled expression deepening. "There are at present twenty-five prisoners in this facility. They are caretakers second. All are double Y chromos—former career criminals, thieves, rapists, murderers, arsonists, child molesters, drug dealers . . . scum." He paused to let the litany sink in.

"But scum that have taken on religion. It may make them appear and sound mellow, but I, for one, don't think it makes them any less dangerous. However, I value its meliorating effect. So I try not to offend their convictions. They appreciate my tolerance and I'm rewarded with a greater amount of peace and quiet than you'd expect to find in a situation like this.

"I don't want to disturb the established order. I don't want ripples in the water. And I most especially don't want a woman walking around giving them ideas and stirring up memories which they have conveniently managed to bury in their respective pasts."

"Yes," Ripley agreed. "Obviously, as you've said, for my own personal safety. In addition to which, despite what you seem to think, I'm not entirely oblivious to the potential problems my temporary presence here creates for you.'

"Exactly."Andrews was clearly pleased by her apparent desire to cooperate. Or in other words, to make life as easy as possible for him. He glanced back at the med tech.

"I will leave the details of the cremation to you, Mr. Clemens." He turned to leave.

"Just one thing, Superintendent."

Andrews halted. "Yes?"

"When I'm done, will you be wanting a time and circumstances report? For the official log, of course."

Andrews pursed his lips thoughtfully. "That won't be necessary, Mr. Clemens. Just 'com me. I'll take care of the rest."

"As you say, Superintendent." Clemens grinned thinly.

· IV ·

Meat. Some of it familiar, some not. Dull rust red struck through with flashes of bright crimson. Small carcasses dangling from old hooks. Huge slabs tipped with protuberant suggestions of amputated limbs, outlined in frozen fat.

Nearby, chickens and cattle, oblivious to their eventual fate. A lone sheep. Live meat.

Most of the abattoir was empty. It had been built to handle the daily needs of hundreds of technicians, miners, and refining personnel. It was far larger than the caretaker prisoners required. They could have left more space between supplies, but the vast rear of the huge chamber, with its echoes of draining blood and slicing and chopping, was a place they preferred to avoid. Too many animate ghosts lingered there, seeking form among milling molecules of tainted air.

The two men wrestled with the cart between them, on which rested the unwieldy carcass of a dead ox. Frank tried to guide it while Murphy goosed forward motion out of the rechargeable electric motor. The motor sputtered and sparked complainingly. When it finally burned out they would simply activate another cart. There were no repair techs among the prison population.

Frank wore the look of the permanently doomed. His much younger companion was not nearly so devastated of aspect. Only Murphy's eyes revealed the furtive nature of someone who'd been on the run and on the wrong side of the law since he'd been old enough to contemplate the notion of working without sticking to a regular job. Much easier to appropriate the earnings of others, preferably but not necessarily without their knowledge. Sometimes he'd been caught, other times not.

The last time had been one too many, and he'd been sent to serve out his sentence on welcoming, exotic Fiorina.

Murphy touched a switch and the cart dumped the clumsy bulk onto the deeply stained floor. Frank was ready with the chains. Together they fastened them around the dead animal's hind legs and began to winch it off the tiles. It went up slowly, in quivering, uneven jerks. The thin but surprisingly strong alloyed links rattled under the load.

"Well, at least Christmas came early." Frank struggled with the load, breathing hard.

"How's that?" Murphy asked him.

"Any dead ox is a good ox."

"God, ain't it right. Smelly bastards, all covered with lice. Rather eat 'em than clean 'em."

Frank looked toward the stalls. "Only three more of the buggers left, then we're done with the pillocks. God, I hate hosing these brutes down. Always get shit on my boots."

Murphy was sucking on his lower lip, his thoughts elsewhere. "Speakin' of hosing down, Frank . . ."

"Yeah?"

Memories glistened in the other man's voice, haunted his face. They were less than pleasant. "I mean, if you got a chance . . . just supposing . . . what would you say to her?"

His companion frowned. "What do you mean, if I got a chance?"

"You know. If you got a chance." Murphy was breathing harder now.

Frank considered. "Just casual, you mean?"

"Yeah. If she just came along by herself, like, without Andrews or Clemens hangin' with her. How would you put it to her? You know, if you ran into her in the mess hall or something."

The other man's eyes glittered. "No problem. Never had any problem with the ladies. I'd say, 'Good day, my dear, how's it going? Anything I could do to be of service?' Then I'd give her the look. You know—up and down. Giver her a wink, nasty smile, she'd get the picture."

"Right," said Murphy sarcastically. "And she'd smile back and say, 'Kiss my ass, you horny old fucker.' "

"I'd be happy to kiss her ass. Be happy to kiss her anywhere she wants."

"Yeah." Murphy's expression darkened unpleasantly. "But treat 'em mean, keep 'em keen . . . right, Frank?"

The older man nodded knowingly. "Treat the queens like whores and the whores like queens. Can't go wrong."

Together they heaved on the chains until the carcass was properly positioned. Frank locked the hoist and they stepped back, letting the dead animal swing in its harness.

Contemplative silence separated the two men for a long moment. Then Frank uttered a casual obscenity. "Frank?"

"Yeah?"

"What do you think killed Babe?" He nodded at the carcass.

Frank shrugged. "Beats me. Just keeled over. Heart attack, maybe."

Murphy spoke from the other side. "How could it have been a heart attack? How old was she?"

"Charts say eleven. In the prime. Tough luck for her, good for us. You know the super won't let us kill any of the animals for meat except on special occasions. So me, I look on this as a bonus for work well done. Chop her up. Later we'll throw her in the stew. Animal this size ought to last for a while. Make the dehys taste like real food."

"Yeah!" Murphy could taste it now, ladled over hot loaves of the self-rising, self-cooking bread from the stores.

Something on the cart caught his attention. Whatever it was, it had been pancaked, flattened beneath the massive bulk of the dead animal. Still discernible was a small, disclike body, a thick, flexible tail, and multiple spidery arms, now crushed and broken. A look of distaste on his face, he picked it up by the tail, the splintered arms dangling toward the floor.

"What's this?"

Frank leaned over for a look, shrugged indifferently. "Dunno. What am I, a xenologist? Looks like some jelly-fish from the beach."

The other man sniffed. The thing had no odor. "Right." He tossed it casually aside.

The leadworks was a kind of liquid hell, a place of fire and simmering heat waves, where both vision and objects wavered as if uncertain of outline. Like much of the rest of the mining facility it had been abandoned largely intact. The difference was that it gave the prisoners something to do, leadworking being considerably less complex than, say, platinum wire production or heavy machinery maintenance. Fiorina's inhabitants were encouraged to make use of the facility, not only to occupy and amuse themselves but also to replace certain equipment as it broke down.

Presently the automatic extruders were drawing molten lead from the glowing caldron into thin tubes which would be used to replace those in an older part of the facility's plant.

The prisoners on duty watched, alternately fascinated and bored by the largely automated procedure. Not only was the leadworks a popular place to work because it offered opportunities for recreation, but also because it was one of the consistently warmest spots in the complex.

"You goin'?" The man who spoke checked two of the simple readouts on the monitoring console. As always, they were well within allowable parameters.

His companion frowned. "Haven't decided. It's nothin' to do with us."

"Be a break in routine, though."

"Still, I dunno'."

A third man turned from the searing caldron and pushed his protective goggles up onto his forehead. "Dillon gonna be there?"

Even as he ventured the query the towering prisoner in question appeared, striding down the metal catwalk toward them.

"Shut it down," he said simply when he reached them. The first prisoner obediently flipped a switch and the caldron immediately began to cool.

"What's the story, man?" asked the man with the goggles, blinking particles from his eyes.

"Yeah," said the prisoner in the middle. "We been talkin' about it, but we ain't been able to decide."

"It's been decided," Dillon informed him. He let his gaze rest on each of them in turn. "We're all goin'. Maybe we didn't know these people, but we show our respect. They wanna burn bodies, that's fine by us, long as it isn't one of us." Having imparted this information, he turned to leave.

The three men followed, the one with the goggles slipping them down around his neck. "Ain't had a funeral in a long time."

. "That's right," agreed his companion somberly. "I've been kind of missing the service. It's so much like a passage, you know? Off this place."

"Amen to that, brother," said the first man, increasing his stride to keep pace with the taller Dillon.

The old smelter creaked and groaned as it was juiced to life. The immense chamber had been cut and blasted out of the solid rock directly above the ore body, then lined where necessary with heat-reflective shielding. Monitors and controls lined the walkways and railings. Cranes and other heavy tracked equipment rested silently where they had been parked by the departing miners. In the shadows thrown by the reduced lighting they resembled Mesozoic fossils escaped from some distant museum.

Flames began to flicker around the beveled edges of the holding pit. They heightened the stark figures of the two prisoners who stood on a crane suspended over the abyss. A pair of nylon sacks hung between them. Their limp contents caused them to sag noticeably in the middle.

Ripley gazed up at the men and their burden, her hands tightening on the rail that separated her from the artificial hell below. Clemens stood next to her, wanting to say something and, as always, failing to find the right words. Having used up all the consolation in his body a number of years ago, he now discovered there was none left for the single forlorn woman standing beside him.

Aaron was there too, and Dillon, and a number of the other prisoners. Despite the fact that the dead man had in fact been something of a government enforcer, none of them smiled or ventured sarcastic remarks. Death was too familiar a companion to all of them, and had been too much of a daily presence in their lives, to be treated with disrespect.

Andrews harrumphed importantly and opened the thin book he carried. "We commit this child and this man to your keeping, O Lord. Their bodies have been taken from the shadow of our nights. They have been released from all darkness and pain. Do not let their souls wander the void, but take them into the company of those who have preceded them."

In the control center below, the prisoner called Troy listened via 'com to the proceedings on the catwalk overhead. When Andrews reached the designated place in the eulogy the prisoner tech began adjusting controls. Telltales shifted from yellow to green. A deep whine sounded behind him, rose to complaining pitch, and died. Other lights flashed ready.

Below the catwalk white-hot flame filled the smelting pit. It roared efficiently, impressively in the semi-darkness. No mountain of ore waited to greet the fire, no crowd of technicians stood ready to fine-tune the process of reducing tons of rubble to slag. The flames seared the sides of the pit and nothing more.

Tears ran slowly down Ripley's cheeks as she stared at the controlled conflagration. She was silent in her sorrow and remembrance, making no noise, issuing no sounds.

There were only the tears. Clemens looked on sympathetically. He wanted to take her in his arms, hold her, comfort her. But there were others present, Andrews among them. He stayed where he was.

"The child and the man have gone beyond our world," Andrews droned on. "Their bodies may lie broken, but their souls are forever eternal and everlasting."

"We who suffer ask the question: Why?" Eyes shifted from the superintendent to Dillon. "Why are the innocent punished? Why the sacrifice? Why the pain?" "There are no promises," the big prisoner intoned solemnly. "There is no certainty. Only that some will be called. That some will be saved."

Up on the crane the rising heat from the furnace finally became too much for the men stationed there. They rocked several times and heaved their burden into the pit, beating a hasty retreat for cooler climes. The sacks fell, tumbling a few times, before being swallowed by the inferno. There was a brief, slightly higher flicker of flame near the edge of the pit as the bags and their contents were instantly incinerated.

Ripley staggered slightly and clutched at Clemens's arm. He was startled but held his ground, giving her the support she needed. The rest of the men looked on. There was no envy in their expressions; only sympathy. Dillon took no notice. He was still reciting.

"But these departed spirits will never know the hardships, the grief and pain which lie ahead for those of us who remain. So we commit these bodies to the void with a glad heart. For within each seed there is the promise of a flower, and within each death, no matter how small, there is always a new life. A new beginning."

*   *   *

There was movement in the abattoir, a stirring amid the dangling carcasses and balletic wraiths of frozen air. The massive corpse of the ox twitched, then began to dance crazily in its chains.

There was no one to witness the gut swelling and expanding until the dead skin was taut as that of a crazed dirigible. No one to see it burst under the pressure, sending bits of flesh and fat flying. Internal organs, liver and stomach, coils of ropy intestines tumbled to the floor. And something else.

A head lifted, struggling upward with spasmodic, instinctive confidence. The compact nightmare turned a slow circle, scanning its surroundings. Hunting. Awkwardly at first but with astonishingly rapid assurance it began to move, searching. It found the air duct and inspected it briefly before vanishing within.

From the time it had emerged from the belly of the ox until its studied disappearance, less than a minute had elapsed.

Upon concluding his speech Dillon bowed his head. The other prisoners did likewise. Ripley glanced at them, then back to the pit where the fires were being electronically banked. She reached up and scratched at her hair, then one ear. A moment later again. This time she looked down at her fingers.

They were coated with what looked like dark, motile dust.

Disgusted, she frantically wiped them clean against her borrowed jumpsuit, looked up to find Clemens eying her knowingly.

"I warned you."

"Okay, I'm convinced. Now what do I do about it?"

"You can live with it," he told her, "or..." He rubbed his naked pate and smiled regretfully.

Her expression twisted. "There's no other way?"

He shook his head. "If there was we'd have found it by now. Not that there's been much impetus to do so. Vanity's one of the first casualties of assignment to Fiorina. You might as well be comfortable. It'll grow back after you leave, and if you don't do anything in the meantime the bugs'll eat the stuff right down to the roots anyway. They may be tiny, but they have large appetites and lousy table manners. Believe me, you'll look worse if you try to ignore it, and you'll scratch yourself silly."

She slumped. "All right. Which way to the beauty parlor?"

The tech was apologetic. "I'm afraid you're talking to it."

The line of shower stalls was stark and sterile, pale white beneath the overheads. Presently all were deserted save one. As the hot, chemically treated water cascaded down her body, Ripley studied herself in the mirror that formed part of one wall.

Strange to be without hair. It was such a slight, ephemeral part of one's body. The only aspect of one's appearance that could be altered easily and at will. She felt herself physically diminished somehow, a queen suddenly bereft of her crown. Yet it would grow back. Clemens had assured her of that. The prisoners had to shave themselves regularly. There was nothing about the bugs or the air that rendered the condition permanent.

She soaped her bare scalp. It was a strange sensation and she felt chilled despite the roaring hot water. The old mining and smelting facility might be short of many things, but water wasn't one of them. The big desalinization plant

down on the bay had been built to provide water for all
installation functions and its full complement of personnel
as well. Even at minimal operational levels it provided more
than enough water for the prisoners to waste.

She shut her eyes and stepped back under the full force
of the heavy spray. As far as she was concerned the past ten
thousand years of human civilization had produced three
really important inventions: speech, writing, and indoor
plumbing.

Outside the stalls, old death and new problems awaited,
though the latter seemed insignificant compared to what
she'd already been through. Clemens and Andrews and the
rest didn't, couldn't, understand that, nor did she feel it
incumbent upon herself to elaborate for them.

After what she'd endured, the prospect of being forced
to spend a few weeks in the company of some hardened
criminals was about as daunting as a walk in the park.

The prisoners had their meals in what had been the
supervisors' mess when the mine had been in operation. The
room still exceeded their modest requirements. But while
the facility was impressive despite having been stripped of
its original expensive decor, the food was something else
again. Still, complaints were infrequent and mild. If not
precisely of gourmet quality, at least there was plenty of it.
While not wishing to pamper its indentured caretakers,
neither did the Company wish them to starve.

Within certain prescribed and well known temporal
parameters the men could eat when they wished. Thanks to
the extra space they tended to cluster in small groups. A few
chose to eat alone. Their solitude was always respected. In
Fiorina's restricted environment enforced conversation was
threatening conversation.

Dillon picked up his preheated tray and scanned the room. Men were chatting, consuming, pretending they had lives. As always, the superintendent and his assistant ate in the same hall as the prisoners, though off to one side. Wordlessly he homed in on a table occupied by three men displaying particularly absorbed expressions. No, not absorbed, he corrected himself. Sullen.

Well, that was hardly a unique situation on Fiorina. Nevertheless, he was curious.

Golic glanced up as the new arrival's bulk shadowed the table, looked away quickly. His eyes met those of his friends Boggs and Rains. The three of them concentrated on their bland meals with preternatural intensity as Dillon slid into the empty seat. They did not object to his presence, but neither did they welcome him.

The four ate in silence. Dillon watched them closely, and they were conscious of his watching them, and still no one said anything.

Finally the big man had had enough. Pausing with his spoon halfway to his mouth, he settled on Boggs.

"Okay. This is eating time, interacting time. Not contemplation seminar. Lotta talk goin' round that we got some disharmony here. One of you guys want to tell me what the problem is?"

Boggs looked away. Golic concentrated on his mash. Dillon did not raise his voice but his impatience was evident nonetheless.

"Speak to me, brothers. You all know me and so you know that I can be persistent. I sense that you are troubled and I wish only to help." He placed a massive, powerful fist gently on the table next to his tray. "Unburden your spirits. Tell me what's the matter."

Rains hesitated, then put down his fork and pushed his

tray toward the center of the table. "All right, you want to know what's wrong? I'll tell you what's wrong. I've learned how to get along here. I never thought that I would but I have. I don't mind the dark, I don't mind the bugs, I don't mind the isolation or all the talk of ghosts in the machinery. But I mind Golic." He waved at the individual in question, who blissfully continued scarfing down his food.

Dillon turned to Boggs. "That the way you feel about it?"

Boggs continued to stir his food nervously, finally looked up. "I ain't one to start something or cause trouble. I just want to get along and serve my time like everybody else."

The big man leaned forward and the table creaked slightly beneath his weight. "I asked you if that's the way you feel about it."

"All right, yeah. Yeah. Hey, the man is crazy. I don't care what Clemens or the 'official' reports say. He's nuts. If he wasn't like this when he got here then he is now. The planet or the place or both have made him like that. He's running on smoke drive, and he smells bad. I ain't goin' outside with him anymore. Not to the beach, not to check the shafts, not nowhere. And ain't nobody can make me," he finished belligerently. "I know my rights."

"Your rights?" Dillon smiled thinly. "Yes, of course. Your rights." He glanced to his left. "You got anything to say for yourself?"

Golic looked up, particles of food clinging to his thick lips, and grinned idiotically. He essayed an indifferent shrug before returning to his meal.

Dillon regarded the other two steadily. "Because Golic doesn't like to talk doesn't mean he's crazy. Just nonverbal. Frankly, from everything I've seen he manages to express what he's feeling as well as anybody else. There are no orators here."

"Get to the point," Boggs mumbled unhappily.

"The point is that he's going with you. He's part of your work team and until further notice or unless he does something more threatening than keep his mouth shut, that's the way it stays. You all have a job to do. Take it from me, you will learn not to mind Golic or his little idiosyncrasies. He's nothing more than another poor, miserable, suffering son of a bitch like you and me. Which means he's no crazier than any of the rest of us."

"Except he smells worse," Rains snapped disgustedly.

"And he's crazy," Boggs added, unrepentant.

Dillon straightened in his seat. "Look, you're making far too much out of this. I've seen it before. It happens when there isn't a whole helluva lot else to do. You start picking on the food, then the bugs, then each other. Golic's different, that's all. No better and no worse than the rest of us."

"He stinks," Rains muttered.

Dillon shot the other man a cautionary look. "None of us is a walking bouquet down here. Knock this shit off. You have a job to do. The three of you. It's a good job."

"Didn't ask for it," Boggs muttered.

"Nobody asks for anything here. You take what's given to you and make the best of it. That way lies survival. For you and for everybody else. This ain't like some Earthside prison. You riot here and no citizen media comes runnin' to listen to your complaints. You just get a lot more uncomfortable. Or you die." Boggs shuffled his feet uneasily.

"Now, listen to me. There's others who'd be willing to take on foraging duty. But in case you ain't noticed, Andrews ain't in a very accommodating mood right now. I wouldn't be asking him about switching assignments and changing rosters." The big man smiled encouragingly. "Hey, you get to work at your own speed, and you're out of sight of the superintendent and his toady. Maybe you'll get lucky, find some good stuff you can try and keep to yourselves."

"Fat chance of that." Rains was still bitter, but less so. Dillon had reminded him of possibilities.

"That's better," said the big man. "Just keep your mind on your work and you won't even notice Golic. You are foragers. You know what that entails. Hunting for overlooked provisions and useful equipment. As we all know from previous scavenging expeditions, Weyland-Yutani's noble, upstanding miners had the useful habit of appropriating their employers' supplies and hoarding them in little private storerooms and cubbies they cut out of the rock in the hopes they could smuggle some of the stuff out and sell it on the open market. They were trying to supplement their incomes. We're interested in supplementing our lives.

"I don't want to hear anymore objections and I don't want to discuss it further. There's tougher duty needs doing if you insist on pressing the matter. You are to do this to help your fellow prisoners. You are to do this to prove your loyalty to me. And I don't want to hear another word about poor Golic."

"Yeah, but—" Rains started to argue. He broke off before he could get started, staring. Boggs looked up. So did Golic. Dillon turned slowly.

Ripley stood in the doorway, surveying the mess hall, which had gone completely silent at her entrance. Her eyes saw everything, met no one's. Stepping over to the food line she studied the identical trays distastefully. The prisoner on serving duty gaped at her unashamedly, his manipulator dangling limp from one hand. Taking a chunk of cornbread from a large plastic basket, she turned and let her gaze rove through the room one more time, until it settled on Dillon.

Andrews and his assistant were as absorbed in the silent tableau as the prisoners. The superintendent watched thoughtfully as the lieutenant walked over to the big man's table and stopped. His knowing expression was resigned as he turned back to his food.

"As I thought, Mr. Aaron. As I thought."

His second-in-command frowned, still gazing across the room at Ripley. "You called it, sir. What now?"

Andrews sighed. "Nothing. For now. Eat your food." He picked up a fork and dug into the steaming brown mass in the center of his tray.

Ripley stood opposite Dillon, behind Boggs. The four men picked at their meals, resolutely indifferent to her presence.

"Thanks for your words at the funeral. They helped. I didn't think I could react like that anymore to anything as futile as words, but I was wrong. I just want you to know that I appreciated it."

The big man gazed fixedly at his plate, shoveling in food with a single-minded determination that was impressive to behold. When she didn't move away he finally looked up.

"You shouldn't be here. Not just on Fiorina . . . you didn't have much choice about that. But in this room. With us. You ought to stay in the infirmary, where you belong. Out of the way."

She bit off a piece of the cornbread, chewed reflectively. For something with a dehy base it was almost tasty.

"I got hungry."

"Clemens could've brought you something."

"I got bored."

Frustrated, he put down his fork and glanced up at her. "I don't know why you're doing this. There's worse things than bein' bored. I don't know why you're talking to me. You don't wanna know me, Lieutenant. I am a murderer and a rapist. Of women."

"Really." Her eyebrows, which she had thinned but not shaved completely, rose. "I guess I must make you nervous."

Boggs's fork halted halfway to his mouth. Rains frowned, and Golic just kept eating, ignoring the byplay completely. Dillon hesitated a moment, then a slow smile spread across his hardened face. He nodded and Ripley took the remaining empty chair.

"Do you have any faith, sister?"

"In what?" She gnawed on the cornbread.

"In anything."

She didn't have to pause to consider. "Not much."

He raised a hand and waved, the expansive gesture encompassing the mess hall and its inhabitants. "We got lots of faith here. Not much else, it's true, but that we got. It doesn't take up much space, the Company and the government can't take it away from us, and every man watches over his own personal store of the stuff. It's not only useful in a place like this, it's damn necessary. Otherwise you despair and in despairing you lose your soul. The government can take away your freedom but not your soul.

"On Earth, in a place like this, it would be different. But this ain't Earth. It ain't even the Sol system. Out here people react differently. Free people and prisoners alike. We're less than free but more than dead. One of the things that keeps us that way is our faith. We have lots, Lieutenant. Enough even for you."

"I got the feeling that women weren't allowed in your faith."

"Why? Because we're all men here? That's a consequence of our population, not our philosophy. If women were sent they'd be invited in. Incarceration doesn't discriminate as to gender. Reason there ain't no women in the faith is that we never had any sent here. But we tolerate anyone. Not much reason to exclude somebody when they're already excluded from everything else by the simple fact of being sent here. We even tolerate the intolerable." His smile widened.

"Thank you," she replied dryly.

He noted her tone. "Hey, that's just a statement of principle. Nothing personal. We got a good place here to wait. Up to now, no temptation."

She leaned back in the chair. "I guess if you can take this place for longer than a year without going crazy, you can take anybody."

Dillon was eating again, enjoying the meal. "Fiorina's as good a place to wait as any other. No surprises. More freedom of movement than you'd have on an inhabited world. Andrews doesn't worry about us going too far from the installation because there's no place to go. It's hard out there. Not much to eat, rotten weather. No company. We're all long-termers here, though not everyone's a lifer. Everyone knows everyone else, what they're like, who can be depended on and who needs a little extra help to make it." He chewed and swallowed.

"There's worse places to serve out your time. I ain't been there, but I've heard of 'em. All things considered, Fiorina suits me just fine. No temptation here."

Ripley gave him a sideways look. "What exactly are you waiting for?"

The big man didn't miss a beat. Or a forkful. "We are waiting," he told her in all seriousness, "for God to return and raise his servants to redemption."

She frowned. "I think you're in for a long wait."

- V -

Later Clemens showed her the assembly hall, pointing out inconsequentials he thought she might find of interest. Eventually they sat, alone in the spacious room. Prisoner Martin quietly swept up nearby.

"How much of the story of this place do you know?"

"What you've told me. What Andrews said. A little that I heard from some of the prisoners."

"Yeah, I saw you talking to Dillon." He poured himself a short whiskey from the metal flask he carried. The distant ceiling loomed above them, four stories high.

"It's pretty interesting, from a psychosocial point of view. Dillon and the rest of them got religion, so to speak, about five years ago."

"What kind of religion?"

Clemens sipped at his liquor. "I don't know. Hard to say. Some sort of millenarian apocalyptic Christian fundamentalist brew."

"Ummmm."

"Exactly. The point is that when the Company wanted to close down this facility, Dillon and the rest of the converts wanted to stay. The Company knows a good thing when it sees it. So they were allowed to remain as custodians, with two minders and a medical officer." He gestured at the deserted assembly hall. "And here we are.

"It's not so bad. Nobody checks on us, nobody bothers us. Regular supply drops from passing ships take care of the essentials. Anything we can scavenge we're allowed to make use of, and the company pays the men minimal caretaker wages while they do their time, which is a damn sight better than what a prisoner earns doing prison work Earthside.

"For comfort the men have view-and-read chips and their private religion. There's plenty to eat, even if it does tend to get monotonous; the water's decent, and so long as you shave regular, the bugs don't bother you. There are few inimical native life-forms and they can't get into the installation. If the weather was better, it would almost be pleasant."

She looked thoughtful as she sipped at her drink. "What about you? How did you happen to get this great assignment?"

He held his cup between his fingers, twirling it back and forth, side to side. "I know you'll find this hard to believe, but it's actually much nicer than my previous posting. I like being left alone. I like being ignored. This is a good place for that. Unless somebody needs attention or gets hurt, which happens a lot less than you might think, my time here is pretty much my own. I can sit and read, watch a viewer, explore the complex, or go into a holding room and scream my head off." He smiled winningly. "It's a helluva lot better than having some sadistic guard or whiny prisoner always on your case." He gestured at her bald pate.

"How do you like your haircut?"

She ran her fingers delicately across her naked skull. "Feels weird. Like the hair's still there but when you reach for it, there's nothing."

He nodded. "Like someone who's lost a leg and thinks he can still feel his foot. The body's a funny thing, and the mind's a heck of a lot funnier." He drained his glass, looked into her eyes.

"Now that I've gone out on a limb for you with Andrews over the cremation, damaging my already less than perfect relationship with the good man, and briefed you on the humdrum history of Fury 161, how about you telling me what you were looking for in that dead girl? And why was it necessary to cremate the bodies?" She started to reply and he raised his hand, palm toward her.

"Please, no more about nasty germs. Andrews was right. Cold storage would have been enough to render them harmless. But that wasn't good enough for you. I want to know why."

She nodded, set her cup aside, and turned back to him. "First I have to know something else."

He shrugged. "Name it."

"Are you attracted to me?"

His gaze narrowed. As he was wondering how to respond, he heard his own voice answering, as though his lips and tongue had abruptly chosen to operate independent of his brain. Which was not, he reflected in mild astonishment, necessarily a bad thing.

"In what way?"

"In that way."

The universe, it appeared, was still full of wonders,

even if Fiorina's perpetual cloud cover tended to obscure them. "You are rather direct. Speaking to someone afflicted with a penchant for solitude, as I have already mentioned, I find that more than a little disconcerting."

"Sorry. It's the only way I know how to be. I've been out here a long time."

"Yes," he murmured. "So have I."

"I don't have time for subterfuges. I don't have time for much of anything except what's really important. I've had to learn that."

He refilled both cups, picked up his own, and swirled the contents, studying the uninformative eddies which appeared in the liquid.

The fan blades were each twice the size of a man. They had to be, to suck air from the surface and draw it down into the condensers which scrubbed, cleaned, and purified Fiorina's dusty atmosphere before pumping the result into shafts and structures. Even so, they were imperfect. Fiorina's atmosphere was simply too dirty.

There were ten fans, one to a shaft. Eight were silent. The remaining pair roared at half speed, supplying air to the installation's western quadrant.

Murphy sang through the respiratory mask that covered his nose and mouth, filtering out surface particles before they were drawn off by the fan. Carbon deposits tended to accumulate on the ductway walls. He burned them off with his laser, watched as the fan sucked them away from his feet and into the filters. It wasn't the best job to have, nor the worst. He took his time and did the best he could. Not because he gave a damn or anticipated the imminent arrival of Company inspectors, but because when he finished with the ducts they'd give him something else to do. Might as

well go about the cleaning as thoroughly as possible so it
would kill as much time as possible.

He was off tune but enthusiastic.

Abruptly he stopped singing. A large deposit had
accumulated in the recess off to his left. Damn storage areas
were like that, always catching large debris that the surface
filters missed. He knelt and extended the handle of the push
broom, winkling the object out. It moved freely, not at all
like a clump of mucky carbon.

It was flat and flexible. At first he thought it was an old
uniform, but when he had it out in the main duct he saw that
it was some kind of animal skin. It was dark and shiny,
more like metal foil than flesh. Funny stuff.

Stretching it out on the floor he saw that it was big
enough to enclose two men, or a young calf. What the
hell . . . ?

Then he knew. There were a few large native animals
on Fiorina; poor, dirt-hugging primitive things with feeble
nervous systems and slow response times. Obviously one
had somehow stumbled into an air intake and, unable to get
out again, had perished for lack of food and water. It
couldn't use the ladders, and the roaring fan constituted an
impenetrable barrier. He poked at the empty skin. This
desiccated husk was all that remained of the unfortunate
visitor. No telling how long it had lain in the recess, ignored
and unnoticed.

The skin looked awfully fresh to have contained an old,
long since dried out corpse. The bugs, he reminded himself.
The bugs would make short work of any flesh that came
their way. It was interesting. He hadn't known that the bugs
would eat bone.

Or maybe there'd been no bones to dispose of. Maybe
it had been a . . . what was the word? An invertebrate, yeah.

Something without bones. Wasn't Fiorina home to those too? He'd have to look it up, or better yet, ask Clemens. The medic would know. He'd bundle the skin up and take it to the infirmary. Maybe he'd made a discovery of some kind, found the skin of a new type of animal. It would look good on his record.

Meanwhile he wasn't getting any work done.

Turning, he burned off a couple of deposits clinging to the lower right-hand curve of the duct. That's when he heard the noise. Frowning, he shut off the laser and flicked on the safety as he turned to look behind him. He'd about decided that his imagination was starting to get to him when he heard it again—a kind of wet, lapping sound.

There was a slightly larger recess a few meters down the duct, a sometime storage area for supplies and tools. It should be empty now, cleaned out, the supplies stocked elsewhere and the tools salvaged by the departing maintenance personnel. But the gurgling noise grew louder the nearer he crept.

He had to bend to see inside. Wishing he had a light, he squinted in the reflected glow from the duct. There was something moving, an indistinct bulk in the darkness. The creature that had shed its skin? If so and he could bring it out alive he was sure to receive an official Company commendation. Maybe his unanticipated contribution to the moribund state of Fiorinan science would be worth a couple of months off his sentence.

His eyes grew accustomed to the weak illumination. He could see it more clearly now, make out a head on a neck. It sensed his presence and turned toward him.

He froze, unable to move. His eyes widened.

Liquid emerged suddenly in a tight, concentrated stream from the unformed monster's mouth, striking the paralyzed prisoner square in the face. Gas hissed as flesh melted on contact with the highly caustic fluid. Murphy stumbled backward, screaming and clawing at his disintegrating face.

Smoke pouring through his clutching fingers, he staggered away from the recess, bouncing off first one wall then the other. He had no thought of where he was going, or where he was. He thought of nothing save the pain. He did not think of the fan.

When he stumbled into the huge blades they shredded him instantly, sending blood and ragged chunks of flesh splattering against the metalwork of the duct. It would have taken some time for his erstwhile friends to have found him if his skull hadn't been caught just right between one blade and the casing. Fouled, the safeties took over and shut down the mechanism. The motor stopped and the blades ground to a halt. Down the main corridor a previously quiet fan automatically picked up the slack.

Then it was quiet again in the side shaft except for the distant, barely audible noise which emerged from the old storage recess, a perverse mewling hiss there was no longer anyone present to overhear.

Clemens's quarters were luxurious compared to those of the other prisoners. He had more space and, as the facility's medical technician, access to certain amenities denied his fellow Fiorinans. But the room was comfortable only by comparison. It would not have passed muster on the most isolated outpost on Earth.

Still, he was aware of his unique position, and as grateful as he could be under the circumstances. Recently those circumstances had become a great deal better than normal.

Ripley shifted beneath the bedsheets of the cot, stretching

and blinking at the ceiling. Clemens stood across the floor, near the built-ins. A narcostick smoked between his lips as he poured something dark and potent from a canister into a glass. For the first time she saw him with his official cowl down. The imprinted code on the back of his shaven skull was clearly visible.

Turning, he saw her looking at him and gestured with the container.

"Sorry I can't offer you a drink, but you're on medication."

She squinted. "What is it this time?"

"It would surprise you."

"I don't doubt it." She smiled. "You've already surprised me."

"Thanks." He held the glass up to the light. "The medical instrumentation the Company left behind is rudimentary, but sophisticated enough in its way. Since we can't always rely on supply drops I have to be able to synthesize quite a range of medications. The program that synthesizes rubbing alcohol doesn't take much adjusting to turn out something considerably more palatable." He sipped at the contents of the glass, looking pleased with himself.

"A small hobby, but a rewarding one."

"Does Andrews know?" she asked him.

"I don't think so. I sure as hell haven't told him. If he knew, he'd order me to stop. Say it was bad for morale and dangerous if the other men knew I could do it. I couldn't disagree with him there. But until he does find out, I'll go on happily rearranging ethyl molecules and their stimulating relations to suit my own personal needs." He held the canister over an open tumbler. "Don't worry. I'll save you some. For later."

"That's thoughtful of you."

"Don't mention it. When I was in school recombinant synthetic chemistry was one of my better subjects." He hesitated. "Speaking of thoughtfulness, while I am deeply appreciative of your attentions, I also realize that they manifested themselves at just the right moment to deflect my last question. In the best possible way, of course. I wouldn't want you to think for a minute that I'd have had it any other way. But the damn thing has a grip on me and won't let loose."

She stared up at him, his glass held delicately in one hand. "You're spoiling the mood."

"That's not my intention. But I'm still a medical officer and one does have a job to do, and frankly, the more effort you put into avoiding the issue, the more curious I am to find out why. What were you looking for in the girl? Why were you so insistent on having the bodies cremated?"

"I get it. Now that I'm in your bed, you think I owe you an answer."

He replied patiently. "Trying to get me mad isn't going to work either. No, you owe me an answer because it's my job to get one and because I stuck my neck out for you to give you what you wanted. Being in my bed has nothing to do with it." He smiled thinly. "Your nonresponsiveness in this matter is likely to complicate our future relationship no end."

She sighed resignedly and turned onto her side. "It's really nothing. Can't we just leave it at that? When I was in deep sleep I had a real bad dream." She shut her eyes against the gruesome memory. "I don't want to talk about it. I just had to be sure what killed her."

She looked back up at the medic. "You have no idea what my recent life has been like or what I've been through. It would make your wildest nightmares seem like the fuzzy musings of an innocent five-year-old. I know that I'll never forget any of it. Never! But that doesn't keep me from trying. So if I seem a little irrational or unreasonably insistent about certain things, try to indulge me. Believe me, I need that. I need someone to be concerned about me for a change. As far as Newt...as far as the girl is concerned, I made a mistake.''

His thumb caressed the side of the small glass he held as he nodded slowly, tight-lipped and understanding. ''Yes, possibly.''

She continued to stare at him. ''Maybe I've made another mistake.''

''How's that?''

''Fraternizing with the prisoners. Physical contact. That's against the rules, isn't it?''

''Definitely. Who was the lucky fellow?''

''You, dummy.''

Clemens eyed her uncertainly. ''I'm not a prisoner.''

She gestured. ''Then what about the code on the back of your head?''

His hand went reflexively to the back of his skull. ''I suppose that does demand an explanation. But I don't think this is the moment for it. Sorry. We are rather spoiling things, aren't we?'' The intercom buzzed for attention. He looked apologetic as he moved to acknowledge the call.

''Got to respond. I'm not allowed the luxury of refusing calls. This isn't Sorbonne Centrale.'' He flicked on the two-way. A thin, poorly reproduced voice filtered through.

''Clemens?''

The medic shot her a resigned look. ''Yes, Mr. Aaron.''

''Andrews wants you to report to Vent Shaft Seventeen in the Second Quadrant. ASAP. We've had an accident.''

Suddenly involved, he turned to make certain the

omnidirectional mike built into the unit got a good dose of his reply. "Something serious?"

"Yeah, you could call it that," the assistant told him. "One of the prisoners on work detail got diced." The unit clicked off abruptly.

"Damn." Clemens drained his glass and set it down on the console, turning back to his guest. "I'm sorry. I have to go. Official duties."

Ripley tensed slightly, fingering the glass. "I was just starting to enjoy the conversation. As opposed to other things."

"How do you think I feel?" he muttered as he popped a closet and began removing clothes.

"Maybe I should come along."

He glanced back at her. "Better that you don't. It's one thing if I'm seen as treating you as part of my regular rounds. If everyone starts noticing us together all the time with you looking decidedly healthy, it might inspire questions. And talk. Among these guys, the less talk the better."

"I understand. I don't like it, but I understand."

He stepped into work trousers. "Those are the two things you have to do to survive on Fiorina. Also, I don't think your presence would be appreciated by Superintendent Andrews. Wait here and take it easy." He smiled reassuringly. "I'll be back."

She said nothing further, looking distinctly unhappy.

There wasn't much to examine. Hell, Clemens thought as he surveyed the carnage inside the air duct, there wasn't much to bury. Cause of death was a foregone conclusion. There were as many stains on the motionless fan as on the walls.

It didn't make a lot of sense. Men regularly stepped on

or brushed against ragged metal edges and cut themselves, or fell off catwalks, or injured themselves trying to body surf in the choppy bay, but they knew intimately the potential dangers of the mothballed mine and studiously avoided them. The giant fan was a threat impossible to dismiss or overlook.

Which didn't necessarily mean the unfortunate and now deceased Murphy was innocent of fooling around. He could have been running, or sliding on the slick ductwork, or just teasing the blades with his broom. He must have slipped, or had part of his clothing caught up in the works. They'd never know, of course. No reason to assign two men to duct cleaning duty. Murphy had been working alone.

Aaron was evidently of similar mind. The assistant was staring grimly at the fan. "He was a nutter. I gave him the assignment. I should've know better, should've sent somebody else, or at least paired him up with someone a little more stable." Behind them prisoner Jude continued to mop up.

Andrews was quietly furious. Not because Murphy was dead, but because of the circumstances. They would not reflect favorably on him. Besides which it would mean more paperwork.

"No apologies, Mr. Aaron. It wasn't your fault. From the look of it, it wasn't anybody's fault except perhaps Mr. Murphy's, and he paid for it." He looked to his medic. "Your observations, Mr. Clemens?"

The tech shrugged. "Not really much to say, is there? Cause of death is unarguably obvious. I doubt he felt any discomfort. I'm sure it was instantaneous."

"No shit." Aaron surveyed the widely scattered human debris with unconcealed distaste.

"I am trying to concoct a scenario," the superintendent continued. "For the report, you understand. I find it difficult to believe that he simply stumbled into so blatant a danger, one in whose proximity he had spent some time working. Perhaps he was pulled in?"

Clemens pursed his lips. "Possible. I'm neither physicist nor mechanic—"

"None of us are, Mr. Clemens," Andrews reminded him. "I am not asking you to render judgment, but simply to offer your opinion on the matter."

The medic nodded. "A sudden rush of air might do it, I would imagine. Power surge resulting in exceptional suction. Only—"

"Right," Aaron said quickly. "Almost happened to me once, in the main quadrant. Four years ago. I always tell people, keep an eye out for the fans. They're so damn big and solid and steady, you don't think of the unexpected happening in their vicinity." He shook his head steadily. "Doesn't matter how much I talk. Nobody listens."

"That's fine," Clemens agreed, "except that before I came down I checked the programming, and the fan was blowing. A power surge should've sent him spinning *up* the duct, not flying into the blades."

Aaron's gaze narrowed, then he shrugged mentally. Let the superintendent and the medic work it out. It was their responsibility. Meant nothing to him. He'd offered his reasoning, done the best he could. He was sorry for Murphy, but what the hell. Accidents happened.

Clemens strolled up the duct tunnel, studying the walls. The bloodstains diminished gradually.

There was a large recess in the left side of the tunnel and he knelt to peer inside. It was a typical ancillary storage chamber, long since cleaned out. As he started to rise and move on, something caught his eye and caused him to hesitate.

It looked like a spill. Not blood. Some kind of chemical discoloration. The normally smooth metal surface was badly pitted.

Andrews had moved up silently to stand nearby. Now he joined the medic in studying the recess. "What's that?"

Clemens straightened. "I really don't know. I just thought it looked funny. Probably been like that ever since the ductwork was installed." His indifference was somewhat forced and the superintendent picked up on it immediately, pinning the medic with his gaze. Clemens looked away.

"I want to see you in my quarters in, say, thirty minutes," he said evenly. "If you please, Mr. Clemens."

He turned toward the rest of the search party, which was busy gathering up the remains of the dead man. "Right. This isn't where I want to spend the rest of my day. Let's finish up and get out so Mr. Troy can restart the unit and we can all get back to normal." He began shepherding the men toward the exit.

Clemens lingered. As soon as he was certain Andrews was fully occupied with concluding the grisly cleanup, the medic returned to his examination of the damaged metal.

It was quiet as a tomb inside the EEV. Shattered consoles clung like pinned arachnids to the walls. Equipment lay where it had fallen from braces or spilled from cabinets. The pilot's chair swung at an angle on its support shaft, like a drunken glove.

A single light illuminated the chaotic interior. Ripley was working inside the burst bulkhead, alternating the laser cutter with less intrusive tools. A protective composite plate peeled away reluctantly to reveal a sealed panel beneath.

Gratified, she went to work on the panel clips, using a special tool to remove them one at a time. The panel itself was clearly labeled.

FLIGHT RECORDER

DO NOT BREAK SEAL

OFFICIAL AUTHORIZATION REQUIRED ISA 445

As soon as the last clip was snapped off she removed the panel and set it aside. Beneath, a smooth-surfaced black box sat snug inside a double-walled, specially cushioned compartment. The compartment was dry and clean, with no lingering smell or dampness to suggest that it had been violated by the intrusive salt water of the bay.

The latch on the side released smoothly and the box face slid aside, revealing readouts and flush-mounted buttons beneath the protective shield. She thumbed one and several telltales lit up instantly. Touching it again, she watched as they shut down.

The box slipped freely out of its compartment. She set it gently on the deck, next to the light, and let her gaze once more rove the devastated interior of the emergency vehicle, trying to remember, trying to forget.

Something moved behind her, scrabbling against the torn and broken superstructure. She whirled, panicky, as her eyes detected movement in the darkness.

"Damn!" she cried, slumping. "You *trying* to scare the life out of me?"

Clemens paused in the cramped entrance, an incongruously boyish grin on his face. "Sorry, but the doorbell isn't working." Straining, he stepped into the chamber. "You know, wandering about without an escort is really going to piss Superintendent Andrews off. Whatever you're up to, putting yourself on his bad side isn't going to help."

"Screw him. What about the accident?" Her tone was intent, her expression earnest.

"Very bad, I'm afraid." He leaned against some dangling wiring, backed off hastily when it threatened to come down around him. "One of the prisoners has been killed."

She looked concerned. "How?"

"It wasn't pretty. Sure you want to know?"

She made a small noise. "If you're worried about me fainting on you, you've got the wrong lady."

"I thought as much. Just giving you the option. It happened in one of the operational air shafts." He shook his head at the memory. "Poor silly bastard backed into a working two-meter high-speed fan. Splattered him all over the place. We had to scrape him off the walls."

"I get the picture. It happens."

"Not here it doesn't. Andrews is ticked. It means he has to file a report."

"By communications beam?"

"No. No need for the expense. I imagine it'll go out with the next ship."

"Then what's he worried about? Nobody'll read it for months."

"You'd have to know the superintendent to understand. He takes everything personal."

"Too bad for him, especially considering his current employment."

Clemens nodded, looking thoughtful. "I found something at the accident site, just a bit away from where it happened. A mark, a burn on the floor. Discolored, blistered metal. It looked a lot like what you found on the girl's cryotube."

She just stared at him, her gaze unblinking, uninformative, her expression unfathomable.

"Look, I'm on your side," the medic insisted when she remained silent. "Whatever it is you're involved in or trying to do, I want to help. But I'd like to know what's going on, or at least what you think is going on. Otherwise I'm not going to be able to be of much use to you. Maybe you can do whatever it is you're trying to do alone. I can't make you talk to me. I just think that I can help, make it easier for you. I have access to equipment. You don't. I have some knowledge that you don't. I won't interfere and I'll rely entirely on your judgment. I have to, since I don't have a clue as to what you're up to."

She paused, considering, while he watched her hopefully. "I hardly know you. Why should I trust you?"

He forced himself to ignore the hurt, knowing there was nothing personal in the query. "No reason. Only that without somebody's help it's going to be hard for you, whatever it is you're trying to do. I hardly know you, either, but I'm willing to follow your lead."

"Why? Why should you? By your own admission you don't have any idea what's going on, what's at stake."

He smiled encouragingly. "Maybe I think I know you a little better than you think you know me."

"You're crazy."

"Is that a hindrance to what you're doing?"

She smiled in spite of herself. "Probably just the opposite. All right." She slid the black box out where he could see it clearly. "I need to know what happened here in the EEV, why we were ejected from our ship while still in deep sleep. If you really want to be helpful, find me a computer with audio and sensory interpretation capabilities so I can access this flight recorder."

Clemens looked doubtful. "We don't have anything like that here. The Company salvaged all the sophisticated cybernetics. Everything they left us is either basic program and response or strictly ROM." He smiled sardonically. "I imagine they didn't want a bunch of dumb prisoners messing with their expensive machinery."

"What about Bishop?"

"Bishop?" He frowned.

"The droid that crashed with me."

"He was checked and discarded as useless."

"Let me be the judge of that." A note of concern entered her voice. "His components haven't been cannibalized or compacted, have they?"

"I told you: nobody here's smart enough to do the first, and there wasn't any reason to waste the energy to carry out the latter. What's left of him's in fewer pieces than the prisoner who got killed, but not many. Don't tell me you think you can get some use out of him?"

"All right, I won't tell you. Where is he?"

Clemens looked resigned. "I'll point you in the proper direction, but I'm afraid I can't join you. I have an appointment. Watch your step, okay?"

She was unfazed. "If I wasn't in the habit of doing so, I'd be dead now twenty times over."

- VI -

The candleworks was more than a hobby. While the installation's sealed, self-contained fusion plant generated more than enough energy to light the entire facility should anyone think it necessary, it provided nothing in the way of portable energy. Rechargeable lights were a scarce and precious commodity. After all, the Company techs whose responsibility it had been to decide what was salvaged and what was left behind had logically assumed that the prisoners wouldn't want to go wandering about the surface of Fiorina at night. Within the installation the fusion plant would provide all the illumination they wanted. And since fusion plants simply did not fail, there was no need to consider, nor were substantial provisions made for, backup.

But there were supplies, secreted by miners or forgotten by the evacuation techs, down in the shafts from which millions of tons of ore had been extracted. Supplies which could make life for prisoners and staff alike a little easier.

There was plenty of time to hunt them out. All that was wanting was portable illumination.

The candleworks solved that, in addition to giving the inhabitants of Fiorina something different to do. There was plenty of the special wax in storage. One of those bulk supplies not worth the expense of shipping it offworld, it had originally been used to make test molds for new equipment. A computer-guided laser Cadcam would model the part and etch the wax, which would then be filled with plastic or carbon composite, and hey presto—instant replacement part. No machinery necessary, no long, drawn-out work with lathes and cutters. Afterward the special wax could be melted down and used again.

The prisoners had no need for replacement parts. What equipment was necessary for their survival was self-contained and functioned just fine without their attentions. So they made candles.

They flickered brightly, cheeringly, throughout the works, dangling in bunches from the ceiling, flashing in lead molds the prisoners had made for themselves. The industrial wax of an advanced civilization served perfectly well to mimic the efforts of a technology thousands of years old.

Prisoner Gregor was helping Golic, Boggs, and Rains stuff the special extra-dense illumination candles into their oversized backpacks. The inclusion of a few carefully chosen impurities helped such candles hold their shape and burn for a very long time. They had no choice but to make use of them, since Andrews would hardly allow use of the installation's irreplaceable portable lights for frivolous activities.

Not that the men really minded. The technology might be primitive, but there was no significant difference in the quality of the illumination provided by the candles and that supplied by their precious few rechargeable fuel cells. Light was light. And there were plenty of candles.

Golic alternated between shoving the squat tapers into his pack and food into his mouth. Particles spilled from his lips, fell into his pack. Rains eyed him with distaste.

"There you are." Gregor hefted one of the bulky packs. "This'll top you off. Golic, don't fidget about. What's all this damn food you've got in here? It's not properly wrapped." The subject of his query smiled blankly and continued to stuff food into his mouth.

Boggs eyed him with disgust. "What the hell does he ever do right?"

Rains snorted. "Eat. He's got that down pretty good."

Dillon and prisoner Junior appeared in the doorway.

"Hey, Golic," the bigger man murmured.

The prisoner thus questioned glanced up and replied through his half-masticated mouthful. "Yeah?"

"Light a candle for Murphy, will you?"

Food spilled from his lips as Golic smiled reassuringly. "Right. I'll light a thousand." He was suddenly wistful. "He was a special friend. He never complained about me, not once. I loved him. Did his head really get split into a million pieces? That's what they're saying."

Dillon helped them slip into the bulky backpacks, giving each man a slap on the shoulder after checking out his individual harness.

"Watch yourselves down there. You've got adequate maps. Use 'em. You find anything that's too big to bring back, make damn good and sure you mark its location so a follow-up team can find it. I remember four years ago a bunch of guys dug out some miner's personal cache of canned goods. Enough to sweeten the kitchen for months.

Didn't mark it right and we never did find the place again. Maybe you three'll get lucky.''

Boggs made a rude noise and there were chuckles all around. ''That's me. Always feeling lucky.''

''Right, then.'' Dillon stepped aside. ''Get goin', don't come back till you find something worthwhile, and watch out for those hundred-meter dropshafts.''

The big man watched them disappear into the access tunnel, watched until distance and curves smothered their lights. Then he and Junior turned and ambled off in the direction of the assembly hall. He had work of his own to attend to.

Andrews's quarters were spacious, if furnished in Spartan style. As superintendent, he'd been given the chambers, which had been the former province of the mine chief. He had plenty of room to spread out, but insufficient furniture to fill the considerable space. Not being a man of much imagination or inclined to delusions of grandeur, he'd sealed most of the rooms and confined himself to three, one each for hygiene, sleeping, and meeting with visitors.

It was the latter activity which occupied him now, as he sat across the modest desk from his single medic. Clemens presented a problem. Technically he was a prisoner and could be treated just like the others. But no one, the superintendent included, disputed his unique status. Less than a free man but higher than an indentured custodian, he earned more than any of the other prisoners. More importantly, they relied on him for services no one else could render. So did Andrews and Aaron.

Clemens was also a cut above the rest of the prison population intellectually. Given the dearth of sparkling conversation available on Fiorina, Andrews valued that ability almost as much as the man's medical talents. Talking with Aaron was about as stimulating as speaking into the log.

But he had to be careful. It wouldn't do for Clemens, any more than for any other prisoner, to acquire too high an opinion of himself. When they met, the two men spun cautious verbs around one another, word waltzing as delicately as a pair of weathered rattlesnakes. Clemens was continually pushing the envelope of independence and Andrews sealing it up again.

The pot dipped over the medic's cup, pouring tea. "Sugar?"

"Thank you," Clemens replied. The superintendent passed the plastic container and watched while his guest ladled out white granules.

"Milk?"

"Yes, please."

Andrews slid the can across the table and leaned forward intently as Clemens lightened the heavy black liquid.

"Listen to me, you piece of shit," the superintendent informed his guest fraternally, "you screw with me one more time and I'll cut you in half."

The medic eased the container of milk aside, picked up his tea, and began to stir it quietly. In the dead silence that ensued, the sound of the spoon ticking methodically against the interior of the ceramic cup seemed as loud and deliberate as a hammer slamming into an anvil.

"I'm not sure I understand," he said finally.

Andrews sat back in his chair, his eyes cutting into his guest. "At 0700 hours I received a reply to my report from the Network. I may point out that to the best of my knowledge this is the first high-level, priority communication this installation has ever received. Even when Fiorina was a working, functioning mining and refining operation it was never so honored. You know why?''

Clemens sipped his tea. ''High-level priority communications have to go through subspace to beat the time problem. That costs plenty.''

Andrews was nodding. ''More than you or I'll ever see.''

''So why rail at me?''

''It's this woman.'' Andrews was clearly troubled. ''They want her looked after. No, more than looked after. They made it very clear they consider her to be of the highest priority. In fact, the communication managed to convey the impression that the rest of the operation here could vanish into a black hole so long as we made sure the woman was alive and in good health when the rescue team arrives.''

''Why?''

''I was hoping you could tell me.'' The superintendent gazed at him intently.

Clemens carefully set his empty cup down on the table. ''I see that it's time to be perfectly frank with you, sir.'' Andrews leaned forward eagerly.

The medic smiled apologetically. ''I don't know a damn thing.''

There was a pause as Andrews's expression darkened. ''I'm glad you find this funny, Clemens. I'm pleased you find it amusing. I wish I could say the same. You know what a communication like this does?''

''Puts your ass in a sling?'' Clemens said pleasantly.

''Puts everyone's ass in a sling. We screw up here, this woman gets hurt or anything, there'll be hell to pay.''

''Then we shouldn't have any trouble arranging compensation, since we all live there now.''

"Be as clever as you want. I don't think the urge will be as strong if something untoward happens and some sentences are extended."

Clemens stiffened slightly. "They're that concerned?"

"I'd show you the actual communication if it wouldn't violate policy. Take my word for it."

"I don't understand what all the fuss is about," Clemens said honestly. "Sure she's been through a great deal, but others have survived deep-space tragedies. Why is the Company so interested in her?"

"I have no idea." Andrews placed his interlocked fingers in front of him. "Why'd you let her out of the infirmary? It's all related to this accident with Murphy somehow. I'd bet my pension on it." He slapped both hands down on the desk. "This is what happens when one of these dumb sons of bitches walks around with a hard-on. Why couldn't you have kept her bottled up and out of sight?"

"There was no reason to. She was healthy, ambulatory, and wanted out. I didn't have either the reason or the authority to restrain her." Clemens's studied savoir faire was beginning to weaken. "I'm a doctor. Not a jailer."

The superintendent's expression twisted. "Don't hand me that. We both know exactly what you are."

Clemens rose and started for the door. Andrews's fingers unlocked and this time he smacked the table with a heavy fist. "Sit down! I haven't dismissed you yet."

The medic replied without turning, struggling to keep himself under control. "I was under the impression I was here at your invitation, not official order. Presently I think it might be better if I left. At the moment I find you very unpleasant to be around. If I remain I might say or do something regrettable."

"You might?" Andrews affected mock dismay. "Isn't

that lovely. Consider this, Mr. Clemens. How would you like me to have you exposed? Though they are a matter of public record elsewhere, up till now the details of your life have been your own here on Fiorina. This personal privilege has facilitated your work with the prisoners, has indeed given you a certain awkward but nonetheless very real status among them. That is easily revoked. If that were to occur I expect that your life here would become rather less pleasant.'' He paused to let everything sink in before continuing.

''What, no witty riposte? No clever jibe? Do I take your silence to mean that you would prefer not to have your dirty little past made part of the general conversation here? Of course, it needn't stop there. Perhaps you'd like me to explain the details of your sordid history to your patient and new friend Lieutenant Ripley? For her personal edification, of course. Strictly in the interests of helping her to allot her remaining time here appropriately.

''No? Then sit the hell down.''

Wordlessly, Clemens turned and resumed his seat. He looked suddenly older, like a man who'd recently lost something precious and had no hope of recovering it.

Andrews regarded his guest thoughtfully. ''I've always been straight with you. I think that's good policy, especially in an environment like we have here. So you won't be particularly upset or surprised when I say that I don't like you.''

''No,'' Clemens murmured in a soft, flat voice. ''I'm not surprised.''

''I don't like you,'' the superintendent repeated. ''You're unpredictable, insolent, possibly dangerous. You have a certain amount of education and are undeniably intelligent, which makes you more of a threat than the average prisoner. You question everything and spend too much time alone.

Always a bad sign. I've survived in this business a long time and I speak from experience. I know what to look for. Your typical incarceree will revolt, sometimes even kill, but it's always the quiet, smart ones who cause the really serious problems.'' He went silent for a moment, considering.

''But you were assigned to this posting and I have to live with that. I just want you to know that if I didn't need a medical officer I wouldn't let you within light-years of this operation.''

''I'm very grateful.''

''How about trying something new, Clemens? Something really different. Try keeping your sarcasms to yourself.'' He squirmed slightly in his chair. ''Now, I'm going to ask you one more time. As your intellectual equal. As someone you respect if not like. As the individual ultimately responsible for the safety and well-being of every man in this facility, yourself included. Is there anything I should know?''

''About what?''

Andrews silently counted to five before smiling. ''About the woman. Don't toy with me anymore. I think that I've made my position clear, personally as well as professionally.''

''Why should I know anything other than the self-evident about her?''

''Because you spend every second you can with her. And I have my suspicions that not all of your concerns are medical in nature. You are far too solicitous of her needs. It doesn't fit your personality profile. You just said yourself that she's fit and able to get around fine on her own. D'you think I'm blind? Do you think I'd have been given this post if I wasn't capable of picking up on the slightest deviations from the norm?'' He muttered to himself. ''Deviates' deviations.''

Clemens sighed. "What do you want to know?"

"That's better." Andrews nodded approvingly. "Has she said anything to you? Not about herself personally. I don't give a damn about that. Wallow in mutual reminiscence all you want, I don't care. I mean professionally. About where she's come from. What her mission was, or is. Most particularly, what the hell was she doing in an EEV with a busted droid, a drowned six-year-old kid, and a dead corporal, and where the hell is the rest of her ship's crew? For that matter, where the hell is her ship?"

"She told me she was part of a combat team that came to grief. The last she remembers was going into deep sleep. At that time the marine was alive and the girl's cryotube was functioning normally. It's been my assumption all along that the girl was drowned and the marine killed in the crash of the EEV.

"I assume beyond that it's all classified. I haven't pressed her for more. She does carry marine lieutenant rank, you know."

"That's all?" Andrews persisted.

Clemens studied his empty teacup. "Yes."

"Nothing more?"

"No."

"You're sure?"

The medic looked up and met the older man's eyes evenly. "Very sure."

Andrews's gaze dropped to his hands and he spoke through clenched teeth. It was obvious there was more, something the medic wasn't telling him, but short of physical coercion there wasn't a damned thing he could do about it. And physical coercion wouldn't work with someone like Clemens, whose inherent stubbornness would keep him from admitting that he had no pride left to defend.

"Get out of here."

Clemens rose wordlessly and started a second time for the door.

"One more thing." The medic paused, looked back to find the superintendent watching him closely. "I take comfort in the daily routine here. So do you. There's a great deal of reassurance to be found in codified monotony. I'm not going to let it be broken. Systematic repetition of familiar tasks is the best and safest narcotic. I'm not going to allow the animals to become agitated. Not by a woman, not by accidents. Not by you."

"Whatever you say," Clemens replied agreeably.

"Don't go getting any funny ideas. Independent action is a valueless concept on Fiorina. Don't think too much. It'll damage your standing in our little community, especially with me, and you'll only end up hurting yourself. You'll do better to keep your long-term goals in mind at all times.

"Your loyalties are to this operation, and to your employer. Not to strangers, or to some misguided notions you may happen to erect on the foundation of your own boredom. She will be gone soon and we will still be here. You and I, Dillon and Aaron and all the rest. Everything will be as it was before the EEV crashed. Don't jeopardize your enviable situation for a temporary abstraction. Do you understand?"

"Yes. Your point is quite clear. Even to someone like me."

Andrews continued to brood uneasily. "I don't want trouble with our employers. I don't want trouble of any kind. I get paid to see that trouble doesn't happen. Our presence here is . . . frowned upon by certain social elements back on Earth. Until the accident we hadn't suffered a death from other than natural causes since the day this group took over caretaking duties from its predecessors. I am aware that it could not have been prevented but it still looks bad in the records. I don't like looking bad, Mr. Clemens." He squinted up at the medic. "You take my meaning?"

"Perfectly, sir."

Andrews continued. "Rescue and resupply will be here soon enough. Meanwhile, you keep an eye on the lieutenant and if you observe anything, ah, potentially disruptive, I know that I can rely on you to notify me of it immediately. Right?"

Clemens nodded briskly. "Right."

Though only partially mollified, the other man could think of nothing more to say. "Very well, then. We understand one another. Good night, Mr. Clemens."

"Good night, Superintendent." He shut the door quietly behind him.

The wind of Fiorina rose and fell, dropping occasionally to querulous zephyrs or rising to tornadic shrieks, but it never stopped. It blew steadily off the bay, carrying the pungent odor of salt water to the outer sections of the installation. Sometimes storms and currents dredged odors more alien from the currents dredged odors more alien from the depths of the sea and sent them spiraling down through the air shafts, slipping through the scrubbers to remind the men that the world they occupied was foreign to the inhabitants of distant Earth, and would kill them if it could.

They went outside but rarely, preferring the familiar surroundings of the immense installation to the oppressive spaciousness of the sullen landscape. There was nothing to look at except the dark waves that broke on the black sand beach, nothing to remind them of the world they had once

known. That was fortunate. Such memories were more
painful than any degree of toil.

The water was cold and home to tiny, disgusting
creatures that bit. Sometimes a few of the men chose to go
fishing, but only for physical and not spiritual nourishment.
Inside the facility it was warm and dry. The wind was no
more than distant, discordant music, to be ignored. Sometimes it was necessary to go outside. These excursions were
invariably brief, and attended to with as much haste as
possible, moving from one refuge to another as quickly as
possible.

In contrast, the figure picking through the sheltered
mountain of debris was doing so with deliberation and care.
Ripley paced the surface of the immense pit, her eyes fixed
on its irregular surface. The original excavation had been
filled in with discarded, broken equipment. She wrestled her
way past monumental components, punctured storage tanks,
worn-out drill bits the size of small trucks, brightly colored
vines of old wiring and corroded tubes.

Wind whipped around outside and she clutched at the
neck of the suit Clemens had found for her. The ruined
mechanical landscape had seemed endless and the cold was
still penetrating her muscles, slowing her and interfering
with her perceptions.

Not to the extent, however, that she failed to see the
expensive silvery filaments protruding from a smaller pim-
ple of recently discarded trash. Kneeling, she began tearing
at the refuse, heaving ruined equipment and bags of garbage
aside to reveal . . .

Bishop.

Or, more accurately, what was left of him. The android
components were scattered amid the rest of the junk and she

had to dig and sort for another hour before she was certain she'd salvaged absolutely everything that might be of use.

She made a preliminary attempt to correctly position the parts. Not only was the result unencouraging, it was downright pitiful. Most of the face and lower jaw was missing, crushed beyond recognition in the EEV or lost somewhere within the mass of trash outside. Portions of the neck, left shoulder, and back had somehow survived intact. In addition there were sensitive related components which had spilled or been torn free from the exterior shell.

Grim-faced and alone, she began carefully packing them into the sack she'd brought with her.

That's when the arm coiled around her neck and the hands grabbed hard at her shoulders. Another hand appeared, clutching feverishly between her legs, fondling roughly. A man materialized in front of her. He was grinning, but there was no humor in his expression.

With a cry she broke free of the arms restraining her. The startled prisoner just gaped as her fist landed in his face and her foot between his thighs. As he crumpled, prisoner Junior appeared and wrapped his thick arms around her, lifting her off the ground to the encouraging sniggers of his companions, throwing her spread-eagled across a corroded pipe. The other men closed in, their body odor obliterating the smell of salt, their eyes glittering.

"Knock it off."

Gregor turned, his gaze narrowing as he isolated a silhouette, close. Dillon.

Gregor forced a grin. "Jump in the saddle, man. You wanna go first?"

Dillon's voice was low, ominous. "I said knock it off."

With his weight resting on the gasping Ripley, Junior

snarled back over his shoulder. "Hey, what's it to you, man?"

"It's wrong."

"Fuck you."

Dillon moved then, deceptively fast. The two men in back went down hard. Junior whirled and brought a huge fist around like a scythe, only to have his opponent weave, gut-punch him, and snatch up a metal bar. Junior staggered and tried to dodge, but the bar connected with the side of his skull. The second blow was harder, and he dropped like stone.

The other cowered and Dillon whacked them again, just to keep them thinking. Then he turned to Ripley, his expression solemn.

"You okay?"

She straightened, still breathing hard. "Yeah. Nothing hurt but my feelings."

"Take off," he said to her. He indicated his fellow prisoners. "I've got to reeducate some of the brothers. We're gonna discuss some matters of the spirit."

She nodded, hefted her bag of Bishop, and started back. As she passed the men on the ground Gregor glanced up at her. She punched him squarely in the mouth. Feeling better, she resumed her course.

- VII -

There is night, which is dark. There is the obdurate emptiness of dreams, whose lights are only imaginary. Beyond all is the void, illuminated however faintly by a million trillion nuclear furnaces.

True darkness, the utter absence of light, the place where a stray photon is as impotent as an atomic anomaly, lies only deep within the earth. "In caverns measureless to man" as the old stanza rhythmically declaims. Or in those cracks and crevices man creates in order to extract the wealth of planets.

A tiny but in and of itself impressive portion of one corner of Fiorina was honeycombed with such excavations, intersecting and crisscrossing like the components of a vast unseen puzzle, their overall pattern discernible only in the records the miners had left behind.

Boggs held his wax-impregnated torch high, waved it around as Rains lit a candle. To such men the darkness was nothing to be feared. It was merely an absence of light. It was also warm within the tunnels, almost oppressively warm.

Rains placed the long-burning taper on the floor, next to the wall. Behind them a line of identical flames stretched off into the distance, delineating the trail they'd taken and the route back to the occupied portion of the complex.

Golic sat down, resting his back against a door set in the solid rock. There was a sign on the door, battered and worn by machinery and time.

TOXIC WASTE DISPOSAL

THIS SPACE HERMETICALLY SEALED

ACCESS TO UNAUTHORIZED PERSONNEL PROHIBITED

That was just fine with the explorers. They had no wish to be suitably authorized.

Rains had unfolded the chart at his feet and crouched, studying the lines and shafts by the light of his torch. The map was no simple matter of vertical and horizontal lines. There were old shafts and comparatively recent ones, fill-ins and reopenings, angle cuts and reduced diameter accessways to accommodate specialized machinery only. Not to mention the thousands of intersecting air ducts. Different colors signified different things.

Numerous earlier expeditions had given the prisoners some idea of what to expect, but there was always the chance that each new team would run into something unexpected. A scrambled byte in the storage units could shift an abyssal shaft ten meters out of line, or into a different tunnel. The chart was a tentative guide at best. So they advanced carefully, putting their faith in their own senses and not in dated printouts.

Boggs leaned close. "How many?" Though he spoke softly, his voice still echoed down the smooth-walled passage.

Rains checked the chart against his portable datapack. "This makes a hundred and eighty-six."

His companion grunted. "I say we call it a vacation and start back."

"No can do." Rains gestured at the seemingly endless length of tunnel that lay before them. "We've at least got to check out the rest of this stretch or Dillon'll pound us."

"What he don't know won't irritate him. I won't tell. How about you, Golic?" The third member of the trio was digging through his backpack. Hearing his name he looked up, frowned, and uttered a low, vaguely inquisitive sound. "That's what I thought."

Golic approached an ancient cigarette machine. Kicking the lock off, he yanked open the door and began loading packs of preserved narcosticks into his duffel. Naturally he chewed as he worked.

On the surface the noise would have been far less noticeable, but in the restricted surroundings and total silence of the tunnel the third man's rumbling maceration resounded like a large, improperly lubricated piece of machinery. Boggs grumbled.

"Can't you chew with your mouth closed? Or better yet, swallow that crap you're eating whole? I'm trying to figure how big this compartment is so we can decide if it's legit toxic storage or some miner's private stock, and I can't think with all the goddamn noise you're making."

Rains rustled the chart disapprovingly. "Just because we're away from the others doesn't mean we should ignore the precepts. You're not supposed to swear."

Boggs's mouth tightened. "Sorry." He stared daggers at Golic, who quite naturally ignored them. Finally he gave up and rose to squint down the tunnel. "We've circled this entire section once. That's all anyone could ask. How many candles, again?'' There was no reply from the floor. "Rains, how many candles?''

His companion wasn't listening. Instead he was scratching himself furiously, an intense nervous reaction that had nothing whatsoever to do with the bugs, who didn't live in the shafts anyway. It was so uncharacteristic, so atypical, that it even managed the daunting task of drawing Golic's attention away from his food. Boggs found himself staring fixedly back the way they'd come.

One by one, the candles which traced their path back to the surface were going out.

"What the shit is doing that?''

Golic pursed his lips, wiping food crumbs from his mouth with the back of one hand. "You're not supposed to swear.''

"Shut up " Not fear—there was nothing to fear in the tunnels—but concern had crept into Boggs's voice "It's okay to say 'shit.' It's not against God.''

"How do you know?'' Golic muttered with almost childlike curiosity.

"Because I asked him the last time we talked and he said it was okay. Now shut up.''

"Dillon'll scream if we don't come back with anything,'' Golic pointed out. The mystery was making him positively voluble. Boggs decided he preferred it when the other man did nothing but eat.

"Let him scream.'' He waited while Rains lit another torch. Reluctantly, Golic repacked his remaining food and rose. All three stared back down the tunnel, back the way they'd come. Whatever was snuffing out the candles remained invisible.

"Must be a breeze from one of the vent shafts. Backwash from the nearest circulating unit. Or maybe a storm on the surface. You know what those sudden downdrafts can do. Damn! If all the candles go out, how're we going to know where we are?''

"We've still got the chart." Rains fingered the sturdy printout.

"You want to rely on that to get us back?"

"Hey, I didn't say that. It's just that we're not lost. Only inconvenienced."

"Well, I don't wanna be inconvenienced, and I don't wanna be stuck down here any longer than absolutely necessary."

"Neither do I." Rains sighed resignedly. "You know what that means. Somebody will have to go back and relight 'em."

"Unless you just want to call it quits now?" Boggs asked hopefully.

Rains managed a grin. "Huh-uh. We finish this tunnel, then we can go back."

"Have it your way." Boggs crossed his arms and succeeded in projecting the air of a man intending to go nowhere fast. "It's your call; you get to do the work."

"Fair enough. Guess I'm nominated."

Boggs gestured at Golic. "Give him your torch."

The other man was reluctant. "That just leaves us here with the one."

"There's nothing wrong with it." Boggs waved the light around to illustrate his point. "And we have the rest of the candles. Besides, Rains'll be right back. Won't you, buddy?"

"Quick as I can. Shouldn't take too long."

"Right, then."

Reluctantly, Golic passed the taller man his light. Together, he and Boggs watched as their companion moved off up the line of candles, pausing to relight each one as he came to it. Each rested where it had been set on the floor. There was nothing to indicate what had extinguished them.

Just a sudden downdraft, Rains told himself. Had to be. Boggs's voice reverberated down the passageway, faint with increasing distance.

"Hey, Rains, watch your step!" They'd marked the couple of vertical shafts they'd passed, but still, if the other man rushed himself in the darkness, disaster was never very far away.

Rains appreciated the caution. You live in close quarters with a very few people for a comparatively long time, you learn to rely on one another. Not that Boggs had reason to worry. Rains advanced with admirable care.

Ahead of him another candle went out and he frowned. There was no hint of a breeze, nothing to suggest the presence of the hypothesized downdraft. What else could be extinguishing the tapers? Very few living things were known to spend much time in the tunnels. There was a kind of primitive large insect that was big enough to knock over a candle, but why a whole row? He shook his head dolefully though there was no one near to observe the gesture. The insect wouldn't move this fast.

Then what?

The tapers he'd reignited burned reassuringly behind him. He straightened. There were no mystical forces at work here. Raising the torch, he aimed it up the tunnel, saw nothing.

Kneeling, he relit the next candle and started toward the next in line. As he did so the light of his torch bounced off the walls, off smooth-cut rock. Off something angular and massive.

It moved.

Very fast, oh, so very fast. Shards of reflection like chromed glass inlaid in adamantine black metal. It made an incongruously soft gurgling sound as it sprang soundlessly toward him. He was unable to identify it, had never seen anything like it, except perhaps in some especially bad dreams half remembered from childhood.

In an instant it was upon him, and at that moment he would gratefully have sought comfort in his worst nightmares.

A hundred meters down the tunnel Golic and Boggs listened to their companion's single echoing shriek. Cold sweat broke out the back of Boggs's neck and hands. Horribly, the scream did not cut off sharply, but instead faded away slowly and gradually like a high-pitched whistle receding into the distance.

Suddenly panicked, Boggs grabbed up the remaining light and took off running, down the passageway, away from the scream. Golic charged after him.

Boggs wouldn't have guessed that he could still move so fast. For a few moments he actually put some distance between them. Then his lack of wind began to tell and he slowed, the torch he clutched making mad shadows on the walls, ceiling, floor. By the time Golic ran him down he was completely exhausted and equally disoriented. Only by sheer good luck had they avoided stumbling into an open sampler pit or down a connecting shaft.

Staggering slightly, he grabbed the other man's arm and spun him around.

Golic gaped in dumb terror. "Didn't you hear it? It was Rains! Oh, God, it was Rains."

"Yeah." Boggs fought to get his breath. "I heard it. He's hurt himself." Prying the torch from the other man's trembling fingers he played it up and down the deserted passageway. "We've got to help him."

"Help him?" Golic's eyes were wide. "You help him. I wanna get out of here!"

"Take it easy. So do I, so do I. First we've got to figure out where we are."

"Isn't that a candle?"

Turning, Boggs advanced a few cautious steps. Sure enough, the line of flickering tapers was clearly visible, stretching off into the distance.

"Damn. We must've cut through an accessway. We ran in a circle. We're back—"

He stopped, steadying the light on the far wall. A figure was leaning there, stiff as anything to be found in cold storage.

Rains.

Staring not back at them but at nothing. His eyes were wide open and immobile as frozen jelly. The expression on his face was not a fit thing for men to look upon. The rest of him was . . . the rest of him was . . .

Boggs felt a hot alkaline rush in his throat and doubled over, retching violently. The torch fell from his suddenly weakened fingers and Golic knelt to pick it up. As he rose he happened to glance ceilingward.

There was something up there. Something on the ceiling. It was big and black and fast and its face was a vision of pure hell. As he stared openmouthed it leaned down, hanging like a gigantic bat from its clawed hind legs, and enveloped Boggs's head in a pair of hands with fingers like articulated cables. Boggs inhaled sharply, gagging on his own vomit.

With an abrupt, convulsive twist the arachnoid horror jerked Boggs's head right off his shoulders, as cleanly as Golic would have removed a loose bolt from its screw. But not as neatly. Blood fountained from the headless torso, splattering the creature, Rains's body, the staring Golic. It broke his paralysis but in the process also snapped something inside his head.

With ghastly indifference the gargoyle tossed Boggs's decapitated skull to the floor and turned slowly to confront the remaining bipedal life-form. Its teeth gleamed like the platinum ingots which had been torn from Fiorina's bowels.

Howling as if all the legions of the damned were after him, Golic whirled and tore down the tunnel. He didn't look where he was going and he didn't think about what he'd seen, and most of all he didn't look back. He didn't dare look back.

If he did, he knew he might see something.

Bishop's remains had been carefully laid out on the worktable. Bright overhead lights illuminated each component. Tools rested in their holders, ready to be called upon. The profusion of torn hair-thin fiber-optic cables was staggering.

Some Ripley had simply tied off as best she could. Her experience did not extend to making repairs on the microscopic level. She'd spent a lot of time wiring the parts together as best she could, sealing and taping, making the obvious connections and hoping nothing absolutely critical lay beyond her limited talent for improvisation.

She wiped her eyes and studied her handiwork. It looked promising, but that meant nothing. Theoretically it stood a chance of working, but then theoretically she shouldn't be in the fix she was in.

No way to know without trying it. She tested the vital connections, then touched a switch. Something sizzled briefly, making her jerk back in the chair. She adjusted a connection, tried the switch again. This time there was no extraneous flash.

Carefully she slipped one bundle of fiber-optic filaments into what she hoped was still a functional self-sorting contact socket. A red digital readout on the test unit nearby immediately went from zero to between seven and eight. As she threw another switch the numbers wavered but held steady.

The android's remaining intact eye blinked. Ripley leaned forward. "Verbal interaction command. Run self-test sequence." Then she wondered why she was whispering.

Within the battered artificial skull something whined. Other telltales on the test unit winked encouragingly. A garbled burbling emerged from the artificial larynx and the collagenic lips parted slightly.

Anxiously she reached into the open throat, her fingers working inside. The burbling resolved itself as the single eye fixed on her face.

"Ripley."

She took a deep breath. She had visual, cognition, coordination, and memory. The external ears looked pretty good, but that signified nothing. All that mattered was the condition of the internal circuits.

"Hello, Bishop." She was surprised at the warmth in her tone. After all, it wasn't as if she were addressing a human being. "Please render a preliminary condition report."

There was a pause, following which, astonishingly, the single eye performed an eloquent roll in its socket. "Lousy. Motor functions are gone, extracranial peripherals nonresponsive, prospects for carrying out programmed functions nil. Minimal sensory facilities barely operative. Not an optimistic self-diagnosis, I'm afraid."

"I'm sorry to hear that," she told him honestly. "I wish it could be otherwise."

"Not as much as I do."

"Can you feel anything?"

"Yes. My legs hurt."

Her lips tightened. "I'm sorry that—"

"It's okay. Pain simulation is only data, which from the rest of my present condition I infer is probably inaccurate. Confirm?"

"I'm afraid so." She managed a weak smile. "I'm afraid that your legs, like most of the rest of you, has gone the way of all flesh."

"Too bad. Hate to see all that quality work lost. Not that it matters in the scheme of things. After all, I'm just a glorified toaster. How are you? I like your new haircut. Reminds me of me before my accessories were installed. Not quite as shiny, though."

"I see that your sense of humor's still intact."

The eye blinked. "Like I said, basic mental functions are still operative. Humor occupies a very small portion of my RAM-interpretive capacity."

"I'd disagree." Her smile faded. "I need your help."

A gurgle emerged from between the artificial lips. "Don't expect anything extensive."

"It doesn't involve a lot of analysis. More straightforward probing. Where I am right now they don't have much in the way of intrusive capability. What I need to know is, can you access the data bank on an EEV flight recorder?"

"No problem. Why?"

"You'll find out faster from the recorder than I could explain. Then you can tell me."

The eye swiveled. "I can just see it. You'll have to use a direct cranial jump, since my auxiliary appendages are gone."

"I know. I'm all set . . . I hope."

"Go ahead and plug in, then."

She picked up the filament running from the black box and leaned toward the disembodied skull. "I've never done this before. It won't hurt or anything?"

"On the contrary, I'm hoping it'll make me feel better."

She nodded and gently inserted the filament into one of several receptacles in the back of his head, wiggling it slightly to make sure the fit was tight.

"That tickles." She jerked her fingers back. "Just kidding," the android told her with a reassuring smile. "Hang on." His eyes closed and the remnants of his forehead wrinkled in concentration. It was, she knew admiringly, nothing more than a redundant bit of cosmetic programming, but it was encouraging to see that something besides the android's basics still functioned.

"I'm home," Bishop murmured several minutes later. "Took longer than I thought. I had to run the probe around some damaged sectors."

"I tested the recorder when I first found it. It checked out okay."

"It is. The damaged sectors are in me. What do you want to know?"

"Everything."

"McNary Flight Recorder, model OV-122, serial number FR-3664874, installed—"

"Are all your language intuition circuits gone? You know what I mean. From the time it was emergency activated. What happened on the *Sulaco*? Why were the cryotubes ejected?"

A new voice emerged from the android's larynx. It was female and mechanical. "Explosive gasses present in the cryogenic compartment. Fire in the cryogenic compartment. All personnel report to evacuation stations." Bishop's voice returned. "There are a large number of repeats without significant deviation in content. Do you wish to hear them all?''

Ripley rubbed her chin, thinking hard. ''No, that's sufficient for now. Explosive gases? Where did they come from? And what started the fire?'' When no response was forthcoming she became alarmed. ''Bishop? Can you hear me?''

There was gurgling, then the android's silky faux voice. ''Sorry. This is harder than I thought it would be. Powering up and functioning are weakening already damaged sectors. I keep losing memory and response capability. I don't know how much longer I can keep this up. You'd better keep your questions brief.''

''Don't null out on me yet, Bishop,'' she said anxiously. ''I was asking you about the report of fire.''

''Fire . . . —*crackle*—* . . . yes. It was electrical, in the subflooring of the cryogenics compartment. Presence of a catalyst combined with damaged materials to produce the explosive gas. Ventilation failed completely. Result was immediately life-threatening. Hence ship's decision to evacuate. EEV detected evidence of explosion on board subsequent to evacuation, with concomitant damage to EEV controls. That's why our landing here was less than perfect. Present status of *Sulaco* unknown. Further details of flight from *Sulaco* to present position available.''

''Skip 'em. Did sensors detect any motile life-forms on the *Sulaco* prior to emergency separation?''

Silence. Then, ''It's very dark here, Ripley. Inside. I'm not used to being dark. Even as we speak portions of me are shutting down. Reasoning is growing difficult and I'm having to fall back on pure logic. I don't like that. It's too stark. Not anything like what I was designed for. I'm not what I used to be.''

"Just a little longer, Bishop," she urged him. She tried tweaking the power up but it did nothing more than make his eye widen slightly and she hastily returned to prescribed levels. "You know what I'm asking. Does the flight recorder indicate the presence of anything on the *Sulaco* besides the four survivors of Archeron? Was there an alien on board? Bishop!"

Nothing. She fine-tuned instrumentation, nudged controls. The eye rolled.

"Back off. I'm still here. So are the answers. It's just taking longer and longer to bring the two together. To answer your question. Yes."

Ripley took a deep breath. The workroom seemed to close in around her, the walls to inch a little nearer. Not that she'd felt safe within the infirmary. For a long while now she hadn't felt safe anywhere.

"Is it still on the *Sulaco* or did it come down with us on the EEV?"

"It was with us all the way."

Her tone tightened. "Does the Company know?"

"The Company knows everything that happened on the ship, from the time it left Earth for Archeron until now, provided it's still intact somewhere out there. It all goes into the central computer and gets fed back to the Network."

A feeling of deadly déjà vu settled over her. She'd battled the Company on this once before, had seen how it had reacted. Any common sense or humanity that faceless organization possessed was subsumed in an all-encompassing, overpowering greed. Back on Earth individuals might grow old and die, to be replaced with new personnel, new directors. But the Company was immortal. It would go on and on. Somehow she doubted that time had wrought any significant changes in its policies, not to mention its corporate morals. In any event, she couldn't take that chance.

"Do they still want an alien?"

"I don't know. Hidden corporate imperatives were not a vital part of my programming. At least, I don't think they were. I can't be sure. I'm not feeling very well."

"Do me a favor, Bishop; take a look around and see."

She waited while he searched. "Sorry," he said finally. "There's nothing there now. That doesn't mean there never was. I am no longer capable of accessing the sectors where such information would ordinarily be stored. I wish I could help you more but in my present condition I'm really not good for much."

"Bull. Your identity program's still intact." She leaned forward and fondly touched the base of the decapitated skull. "There's still a lot of Bishop in there. I'll save your program. I've got plenty of storage capacity available here. If I ever get out of this I'll make sure you come with me. They can wire you up again."

"How are you going to save my identity? Copy it into standard chip-ROM? I know what that's like. No sensory input, no tactile output. Blind, deaf, dumb, and immobile. Humans call it limbo. Know what we androids call it? Gumbo. Electronic gumbo. No, thanks. I'd rather go null than nuts."

"You won't go nuts, Bishop. You're too tough for that."

"Am I? I'm only as tough as my body and my programming. The former's gone and the latter's fading fast. I'd rather be an intact memory than a desiccated reality. I'm tired. Everything's slipping away. Do me a favor and just disconnect. It's possible I could be reworked, installed in a new body, but there'd be omphalotic damage, maybe identity loss as well. I'd never be top of the line again. I'd rather not have to deal with that. Do you understand what it means, to look forward only to being less than you were? No, thanks. I'd rather be nothing.''

She hesitated. "You're sure?"

"Do it for me, Ripley. You owe me."

"I don't owe you anything, Bishop. You're just a machine."

"I saved you and the girl on Archeron. Do it for me . . . as a friend."

Reluctantly, she nodded. The eye winked a last time, then closed peacefully. There was no reaction, no twitching or jerking when she pulled the filaments. Once more the head lay motionless on the worktable.

"Sorry, Bishop, but you're like an old calculator. Friendly and comfortable. If you can be repaired, I'm going to see to it that that comes to pass. If not, well, sleep peacefully wherever it is that androids sleep, and try not to dream. If things work out, I'll get back to you later."

Her gaze lifted and she found herself staring at the far wall. A single holo hung there. It showed a small thatched cottage nestled amid green trees and hedges. A crystalline blue-green stream flowed past the front of the cottage and clouds scudded by overhead. As she watched, the sky darkened and a brilliant sunset appeared above the house.

Her fingers fumbled along the tabletop until they closed around a precision extractor. Flung with all the considerable force of which she was capable and accelerated by her cry of outrage and frustration, it made a most satisfying noise as it reduced the impossibly bucolic simulation to glittering fragments.

*   *   *

Most of the blood on Golic's jacket and face had dried to a thick, glutinous consistency, but some was still liquid enough to drip onto the mess hall table. He ate quietly, spooning up the crispy cereal. Once, he paused to add some sugar from a bowl. He stared straight at the dish but did not see it. What he saw now was very private and wholly internalized.

The day cook, who's name was Eric, entered with a load of plates. As he started toward the first table he caught sight of Golic and stopped. And stared. Fortunately the plates were unbreakable. It was hard to get things like new plates on Fiorina.

''Golic?'' he finally murmured. The prisoner at the table continued to eat and did not look up.

The sound of the crashing dishes brought others in: Dillon, Andrews, Aaron, Morse, and a prisoner named Arthur. They joined the stupefied cook in staring at the apparition seated alone at the table.

Golic finally noticed all the attention. He looked up and smiled.

Blankly.

Ripley was sitting alone in the rear of the infirmary when they brought him in. She watched silently as Dillon, Andrews, Aaron, and Clemens walked the straightjacketed Golic over to a bed and eased him down. His face and hair were spotted with matted blood, his eyes in constant motion as they repeatedly checked the ventilator covers, the ceiling, the door.

Clemens did his best to clean him up, using soft towels, mild solvent, and disinfectant. Golic looked to be in much worse shape than he actually was. Physically, anyway. It was left to Andrews, Aaron, and Dillon to tie him to the cot. His mouth remained unrestrained.

''Go ahead, don't listen to me. Don't believe me. It

doesn't matter. Nothing matters anymore. You pious assholes are all gonna die. The Beast has risen and it feeds on human flesh. Nobody can stop it. The time has come." He turned away from the superintendent, staring straight ahead. "I saw it. It looked at me. It had no eyes, but it looked at me."

"What about Boggs and Rains?" Dillon asked evenly. "Where are they? What's happened to them?"

Golic blinked, regarded his interrogators unrepentantly. "I didn't do it. Back in the tunnel. They never had a chance, not a chance. There was nothing I could do but save myself. The dragon did it. Slaughtered 'em like pigs. It wasn't me. Why do I get blamed for everything? Nobody can stop it." He began to laugh and cry simultaneously. "Not a chance, no, no, not a chance!" Clemens was working on the back of his head now.

Andrews studied the quivering remains of what had once been a human being. Not much of a human being, true, but human nonetheless. He was not pleased, but neither was he angry. There was nothing here to get angry at.

"Stark raving mad. I'm not saying it was anyone's fault, but he should have been chained up. Figuratively speaking, of course." The superintendent glanced at his medic. "Sedated. You didn't see this coming, Mr. Clemens?"

"You know me, sir. I don't diagnose. I only pre- scribe." Clemens had almost finished his cleaning. Golic looked better, but only if you avoided his eyes.

"Yes, of course. Precognitive psychology isn't your specialty, is it? If anyone should have taken note, it was me."

"Don't blame yourself, sir," said Aaron.

"I'm not. Merely verbalizing certain regrets. Some- times insanity lurks quiet and unseen beneath the surface of a man, awaiting only the proper stimulus for it to burst forth. Like certain desert seeds that propagate only once every ten or eleven years, when the rains are heavy enough." He sighed. "I would very much like to see a normal, gentle rain again."

"Well, you called it right, sir," Aaron continued. "He's mad as a fuckin' hatter."

"I do so delight in the manner in which you enliven your everyday conversation with pithy anachronisms, Mr. Aaron." Andrews looked to his trustee. "He seems to be calming down a little. Permanent tranquilization is an expensive proposition and its use would have to be justified in the record. Let's try keeping him separated from the rest for a while, Mr. Dillon, and see if it has a salutary effect. I don't want him causing a panic. Clemens, sedate this poor idiot sufficiently so that he won't be a danger to himself or to anyone else. Mr. Dillon, I'll rely on you to keep an eye on him after he's released. Hopefully he will improve. It would make things simpler."

"Very well, Superintendent. But no full sedation until we know about the other brothers."

"You ain't gonna get anything out of that." Aaron gestured disgustedly at the straightjacket's trembling inhabitant.

"We have to try." Dillon leaned close, searching his fellow prisoner's face. "Pull yourself together, man. Talk to me. Where are the brothers? Where are Rains and Boggs?"

Golic licked his lips. They were badly chewed and still bled slightly despite Clemens's efficient ministrations. "Rains?" he whispered, his brow furrowing with the effort of trying to remember. "Boggs?" Suddenly his eyes widened afresh and he looked up sharply, as if seeing them for the first time. "I didn't do it! It wasn't me. It was . . . it was . . ." He started sobbing again, bawling and babbling hysterically.

Andrews looked on, shaking his head sadly. "Hopeless. Mr. Aaron's right. You're not going to get anything out of him for a while, if ever. We're not going to wait until we do."

Dillon straightened. "It's your call, Superintendent."

"We'll have to send out a search party. Sensible people who aren't afraid of the dark or each other. I'm afraid we have to assume that there is a very good chance this simple bastard has murdered them." He hesitated. "If you are at all familiar with his record, then you know that such a scenario is not beyond the realm of possibility."

"You don't know that, sir," said Dillon. "He never lied to me. He's crazy. He's a fool. But he's not a liar."

"You are well-meaning, Mr. Dillon, but overly generous to a fellow prisoner." Andrews fought back the sarcasm which sprang immediately to mind. "Personally I'd consider Golic a poor vessel for your trust."

Dillon's lips tightened. "I'm not naive, sir. I know enough about him to want to keep an eye on him as much as help him."

"Good. I don't want any more people vanishing because of his ravings."

Ripley rose and approached the group. All eyes turned to regard her.

"There's a chance he's telling the truth." Clemens gaped at her. She ignored him. "I need to talk to him about this dragon."

Andrews's reply was crisp. "You're not talking to anyone, Lieutenant. I am not interested in your opinions because you are not in full possession of the facts." He gestured toward Golic. "This man is a convicted multiple murderer, known for particularly brutal and ghastly crimes."

"I didn't do it!" the man in the straightjacket burbled helplessly.

Andrews looked around. "Isn't that right, Mr. Dillon?"

"Yeah," Dillon agreed reluctantly, "that part's right."

Ripley gazed hard at the superintendent. "I need to talk to you. It's important."

The older man considered thoughtfully. "When I have finished with my official duties I'll be quite pleased to have a little chat. Yes?"

She looked as if she wanted to say something further, but simply nodded.

- VIII -

Aaron took charge of the water pitcher, making sure the glasses were filled. He needn't have bothered. Once Ripley started talking, no one noticed irrelevant details such as thirst.

She explained carefully and in detail, leaving nothing out, from the time the original alien eggs had been discovered in the hold of the gigantic ship of still unknown origin on Archeron, to the destruction of the original crew of the *Nostromo* and Ripley's subsequent escape, to the later devastating encounter on Archeron and her flight from there in the company of her now dead companions.

Her ability to recall every relevant incident and detail might have struck an observer as prodigious, but remembering was not her problem. What tormented her daily was her inability to forget.

It was quiet in the superintendent's quarters for quite a

while after she finished. Ripley downed half her glass of purified water, watching his face.

He laced his fingers over his belly. "Let me see if I have this correct, Lieutenant. What you say we're dealing with here is an eight-foot-tall carnivorous insect of some kind with acidic body fluids, and that it arrived on your spaceship."

"We don't know that it's an insect," she corrected him. "That's the simplest and most obvious analog, but nobody knows for sure. They don't lend themselves to easy taxonomic study. It's hard to dissect something that dissolves your instruments after it's dead and tries to eat or impregnate you while it's alive. The colony on Archeron devoted itself frantically to such studies. It didn't matter. The creatures wiped them out before they could learn anything. Unfortunately, their records were destroyed when the base fusion planet went critical. We know a little about them, just enough to make a few generalizations.

"About all we can say with a reasonable degree of assurance is that they have a biosocial system crudely analogous to the social insects of Earth, like the ants and the bees and so forth. Beyond that, nobody knows anything. Their intelligence level is certainly much greater than that of any social arthropod, though at this point it's hard to say whether they're capable of higher reasoning as we know it. I'm almost certain they can communicate by smell. They may have additional perceptive capabilities we know nothing about.

"They're incredibly quick, strong, and tough. I personally watched one survive quite well in deep interstellar vacuum until I could fry it with an EEV's engines."

"And it kills on sight and is generally unpleasant," Andrews finished for her. "So you claim. And of course you expect me to accept this entire fantastic story solely on your word.''

"Right, sir," said Aaron quickly, "that's a beauty. Never heard anything like it, sir.''

"No, I don't expect you to accept it," Ripley replied softly. "I've dealt with people like you before.''

Andrews replied without umbrage. "I'll ignore that. Assuming for the moment that I accept the gist of what you've said, what would you suggest we do? Compose our wills and wait to be eaten?''

"For some people that might not be a bad idea, but it doesn't work for me. These things can be fought. They can be killed. What kind of weapons have you got?''

Andrews unlocked his fingers and looked unhappy. "This is a prison. Even though there's nowhere for anyone to escape to on Fiorina, it's not a good idea to allow prisoners access to firearms. Someone might get the idea they could use them to take over the supply shuttle, or some similar crackbrained idea. Removing weapons removes the temptations to steal and use them.''

"No weapons of any kind?''

"Sorry. This is a modern, civilized prison facility. We're on the honor system. The men here, though extreme cases, are doing more than just paying their debts to society. They're functioning as active caretakers. The Company feels that the presence of weapons would intimidate them, to the detriment of their work. Why do you think there are only two supervisors here, myself and Aaron? If not for the system, we couldn't control this bunch with twenty supervisors and a complete arsenal." He paused thoughtfully.

"There are some large carving knives in the abattoir, a few more in the mess hall and kitchen. Some fire axes scattered about. Nothing terribly formidable.''

Ripley slumped in her chair, muttering disconsolately. "Then we're fucked."

"No, you're fucked," the superintendent replied calmly. "Confined to the infirmary. Quarantined."

She gaped at him. "But why?"

"Because you've been a problem ever since you showed up here, and I don't want that problem compounded. It's my responsibility to deal with this now, whatever it is, and I'll rest easier knowing where you are at all times. The men are going to be nervous enough as it is. Having you floating around at your leisure poking into places you shouldn't will be anything but a stabilizing influence."

"You can't do this. I've done nothing wrong."

"I didn't say that you had. I'm confining you for your own safety. I'm in charge here and I'm exercising my discretion as installation superintendent. Feel free to file an official complaint with a board of inquiry when you get back." He smiled paternally.

"You'll have it all to yourself, Lieutenant. I think you'll be safe from any large nasty beasts while you're there. Right? Yes, that's a good girl. Mr. Aaron will escort you."

Ripley rose. "You're making a bad decision."

"Somehow I think I'll manage to live with it. Aaron, after escorting the lieutenant to her new quarters, get going on organizing a search party. Fast. Right now all we have to go on is that babbling Golic. Boggs and Rains may only be injured and waiting for help."

"Right, sir."

"You're all wrong on this, Andrews," Ripley told him. "All wrong. You're not going to find anybody alive in those tunnels."

"We'll see." He followed her with his eyes as his assistant guided her out.

She sat on the cot, sullen and angry. Clemens stood nearby, eyeing her. Aaron's voice sounding over the intercom system made her look up.

"Let's all report to the mess hall. Mr. Andrews wants a meeting. Mess hall, right away, gang." A subtle electronic hum punctuated the second-in-command's brief announcement.

Ripley looked over at the medical officer. "Isn't there any way off Fiorina? An emergency service shuttle? Some damned way to escape?"

Clemens shook his head. "This is a prison now, remember? There's no way out. Our supply ship comes once every six months."

"That's it?" She slumped.

"No reason to panic. They are sending someone to pick you up and investigate this whole mess. Quite soon, I gather."

"Really? What's soon?"

"I don't know." Clemens was clearly bothered by something other than the unfortunate Murphy's death. "No one's ever been in a hurry to get here before. It's always the other way 'round. Diverting a ship from its regular run is difficult, not to mention expensive as hell. Do you want to tell me what you and Andrews talked about?"

She looked away. "No, I don't. You'd just think I was crazy." Her attention wandered to the far corner where the catatonic Golic stood staring blankly at the wall. He looked a lot better since Clemens had cleaned him up.

"That's a bit uncharitable," the med tech murmured. "How are you feeling?"

Ripley licked her lips. "Not so hot. Nauseous, sick to my stomach. And pissed off."

He straightened, nodding to himself. "Shock's starting to set in. Not unexpected, given what you've been through recently. It's a wonder you're not over there sharing a blank wall with Golic." Walking over, he gave her a cursory examination, then headed for a cabinet, popped the catch, and began fumbling with the contents.

"I'd best give you another cocktail."

She saw him working with the injector. "No. I need to stay alert." Her eyes instinctively considered possible entrances: the air vents, the doorway. But her vision was hazy, her thoughts dulled.

Clemens came toward her, holding the injector in one hand. "Look at you. Call that alert? You're practically falling over. The body's a hell of an efficient machine, but it's still just a machine. Ask too much of it and you risk overload."

She shoved back a sleeve. "Don't lecture me. I know when I'm pushing things. Just give me the stuff."

The figure in the corner was mumbling aloud. "I don't know why people blame me for things. Weird, isn't it? It's not like I'm perfect or something but, sweet William, I don't see where some people come off always blaming others for life's little problems."

Clemens smiled. "That's quite profound. Thank you, Golic." He filled the injector, checking the level.

As she sat there waiting to receive the medication she happened to glance in Golic's direction and was surprised to see him grinning back at her. His expression was inhuman, devoid of thought—a pure idiot's delight. She looked away distastefully, her mind on matters of greater import.

''Are you married?'' the straightjacketed hulk asked unexpectedly.

Ripley started. ''Me?''

''You should get married.'' Golic was utterly serious. ''Have kids . . . pretty girl. I know lots of 'em. Back home. They always like me. You're gonna die too.'' He began to whistle to himself.

''Are you?'' Clemens inquired.

''What?''

''Married.''

''Why?''

''Just curious.''

''No.'' He came toward her, the injector hanging from his fingers. ''How about leveling with me?''

He hesitated. ''Could you be a little more specific?''

''When I asked you how you got assigned here you avoided the question. When I asked you about the prison ID tattoo on the back of your head you ducked me again.''

Clemens looked away. ''It's a long sad story. A bit melodramatic, I'm afraid.''

''So entertain me.'' She crossed her arms over her chest and settled back on the cot.

''Well, my problem was that I was smart. Very smart. I knew everything, you see. I was brilliant and therefore thought I could get away with anything. And for a while I did.

''I was right out of med school, during which time I had managed the extraordinary accomplishment of finishing in the top five percent of my class despite having acquired what I confidently believed to be a tolerable addiction to Midaphine. Do you know that particular pharmaceutical?'' Ripley shook her head slowly.

''Oh, it's a lovely chain of peptides and such, it is.

Makes you feel like you're invincible without compromising your judgment. It does demand that you maintain a certain level in your bloodstream, though. Clever fellow that I was, I had no trouble appropriating adequate supplies from whatever facility I happened to be working in at the time.

"I was considered most promising, a physician-to-be of exceptional gifts and stamina, insightful and caring. No one suspected that my primary patient was always myself.

"It happened during my first residency. The center was delighted to have me. I did the work of two, never complained, was almost always correct in my diagnoses and prescriptions. I did a thirty-six-hour stretch in an ER, went out, got high as an orbital shuttle, was crawling into bed to lose myself in the sensation of floating all night, when the 'com buzzed.

"A pressure unit had blown on the center's fuel station. Everyone they could get hold of was called in to help. Thirty seriously injured but only a few had to be sent to intensive care. The rest just needed quick but rote attention. Nothing complicated. Nothing a halfway competent intern couldn't have managed. I figured I'd take care of it myself and then hiphead it back home before anyone noticed that I was awfully bright and cheery for someone who'd just been yanked out of the sack at three in the morning." He paused a moment to gather his thoughts.

"Eleven of the thirty died when I prescribed the wrong dosage of painkiller. Such a small thing. Such a simple thing. Any fool could've handled it. Any fool. That's Midaphine for you. Hardly ever affects your judgment. Only once in a while."

"I'm sorry," she said softly.

"Don't be." His expression was unforgiving. "No one else was. I got seven years in prison, lifetime probation, and my license permanently reduced to a 3-C, with severe restrictions on what and where I could practice. While in prison I kicked my wonderful habit. Didn't matter. Too many relatives around who remembered their dead. I never had a chance of getting the restrictions revised. I embarrassed my profession, and the examiners delighted in making an example of me. After that you can imagine how many outfits were eager to employ someone with my professional qualifications. So here I am."

"I'm still sorry."

"For me? Or about what happened? If it's the latter, so am I. About the prison sentence and subsequent restrictions, no. I deserved it. I deserved everything that's happened to me. I wiped out eleven lives. Casually, with a dumb smile on my face. I'm sure that the people I killed had promising careers as well. I destroyed eleven families. And while I can't ever forget, I've learned to live with it. That's one positive thing about being assigned to a place like this. It helps you learn how to live with things that you've done."

"Did you serve time here?"

"Yes, and I got to know this motley crew quite well. So when they stayed, I stayed. Nobody else would employ me." He moved to give her the injection. "So, will you trust me with an injector?"

As he was leaning toward her the alien hit the floor behind him as silently as it fell from the ceiling, landing in a supportive crouch and straining to its full height. It was astonishing and appalling how something that size could move so quietly. She saw it come erect, towering over the smiling medic, metallic incisors gleaming in the pale over-head light.

Even as she fought to make her paralyzed vocal cords function, part of her noted that it was slightly different in appearance from every alien type she had encountered previously. The head was fuller, the body more massive. The more subtle physical discrepancies registered as brief, observational tics in the frozen instant of horror.

Clemens leaned toward her, suddenly more than merely concerned. "Hey, what's wrong? You look like you're having trouble breathing. I can—"

The alien ripped his head off and flung it aside. Still she didn't scream. She wanted to. She tried. But she couldn't. Her diaphragm pushed air but no sound.

It shoved Clemens's spurting corpse aside and gazed down at her. If only it had eyes, a part of her thought, instead of visual perceptors as yet unstudied. No matter how horrible or bloodshot, at least you could connect with an eye. The windows of the soul, she'd read somewhere.

The alien had no eyes and, quite likely, no soul.

She started to shiver. She'd run from them before, and fought them before, but in the enclosed confines of the tomblike infirmary there was nowhere to run and nothing to fight with. It was all over. A part of her was glad. At least there would be no more nightmares, no more waking up screaming in strange beds. There would be peace.

"Hey, you, get over here!" Golic suddenly shouted. "Lemmee loose. I can help you. We can kill all these assholes."

The Boschian vision turned slowly to regard the prisoner. Then it looked once more at the immobile woman on the bed. With a singular leap it flung itself at the ceiling, cablelike fingers grasping the edge of the gaping air duct through which it had arrived, and was gone. Skittering sounds echoed from above, quickly fading into the distance.

Ripley didn't move. Nothing had happened. The beast hadn't touched her. But then, she understood virtually nothing about them. Something about her had put it off. Perhaps they wouldn't attack the unhealthy. Or maybe it had been something in Golic's manner.

Though still alive, she wasn't sure whether to be grateful or not.

- IX -

Andrews stood before his charges in the mess hall, silently surveying their expectant, curious faces while Dillon prepared to give his traditional invocation. Aaron sat nearby, wondering what his boss had on his mind.

"All rise, all pray. Blessed is the Lord." The prisoners complied, striking reverent attitudes. Dillon continued.

"Give us the strength, O Lord, to endure. We recognize we are poor sinners in the hands of an angry God. Let the circle be unbroken, until the day. Amen." Each prisoner raised his right fist, then took a seat.

As Dillon surveyed them his formerly beatific expression twisting with appalling suddenness.

"What the fuck is happening here? What is this bullshit that's coming down? We got murder! We got rape! We got brothers in trouble! I don't want no more bullshit around here! We got problems, we stand together."

Andrews let the silence that followed Dillon's outburst

linger until he was confident he had everyone's attention. He cleared his throat ceremoniously.

"Yes, thank you, Mr. Dillon," he began in his usual no-nonsense tone. "All right. Once again this is rumor control. Here are the facts."

"At 0400 hours prisoner Murphy, through carelessness and probably a good dose of stupidity on his part, was found dead in Vent shaft Seventeen. From the information gathered on the spot it would appear that he was standing too close to the ventilator fan when a strong downdraft struck, and was consequently sucked or blown into the blades. Medical Officer Clemens acted as coroner on the occasion and his official report is as straightforward as you might expect as to cause of death."

Several of the prisoners murmured under their breath. Andrews eyed them until they were quiet once more.

He began to pace as he spoke. "Not long thereafter prisoners Boggs, Rains, and Golic left on a routine forage and scavenge mission into the shafts. They were well equipped and presumably knew what they were about."

"I can confirm that," Dillon put in.

Andrews acknowledged the big man's comment with a glance, resumed his declamation. "At about 0700 hours prisoner Golic reappeared in a deranged state. He was covered with blood and babbling nonsense. Presently he is physically restrained and receiving medical treatment in the infirmary. Prisoners Boggs and Rains are still missing. We are forced to consider the possibility that they have met with foul play at the hands of prisoner Golic." He paused to let that sink in.

"The history of the prisoner in question is not incompatible with such a suspicion. While no one is sent here who has not first been treated and cleared by Rehabilitation

Central on Earth, not every program of treatment is perfect or everlasting.''

"I heard that," said Dillon.

"Just so. However, until prisoners Rains and Boggs, or their bodies, are located and the reason for their absence resolved, any conclusions are necessarily premature. They may be sitting in one of the tunnels, injured and unable to move, waiting for help to arrive. Or they may have gotten lost trying to find their way out. Obviously there is an urgent need to organize and send out a search party. Volunteers will be appreciated and the offer appropriately noted in your records." He stopped in front of the north wall, which had been fashioned of locally poured lead.

"I think it's fair to say that our smoothly running facility has suddenly developed a few problems. It is no cause for panic or alarm and in fact is to be occasionally expected in a situation like this. Whatever the eventual resolution of this particular unfortunate incident I think that I may safely say a return to normal operations can be anticipated within a very short while.

"In the meantime we must all keep our wits about us and pull together for the next few days, until the rescue team arrives to pick up Lieutenant Ripley. I may even go so far as to say that her unplanned arrival here, while creating some problems of its own, has likewise caused the Company to divert a ship to Fiorina. That means the possibility of obtaining extra supplies and perhaps a few luxuries well ahead of schedule. It is something to look forward to. So we should all be looking to the days ahead with anticipation."

The door to his right slammed open to admit Ripley.

Out of breath and anxious, she ignored the stares of everyone present.

"It's here! It got Clemens!" She was glancing around wildly, her eyes inspecting the dark corners and distant corridors of the assembly hall.

The veins bulged in Andrews's neck. "Lieutenant, I've had about enough of you. Stop this raving at once! Stop it! You're spreading panic unnecessarily and without proof, and I won't have it, you hear me? I won't have it!"

She glared at him. "I'm telling you, it's here!"

"And I'm telling you, get control of yourself, Lieutenant!" He looked sharply to his right. "Mr. Aaron, get that foolish woman under control at once. Get her back to the infirmary!"

"Yes, sir." Aaron took a step toward Ripley. Her expression made him hesitate. She looked no less physically capable than the average prisoner.

As he considered what to do next the lights suddenly flickered wildly. Prisoners shouted, ran into one another, looked around in confusion. Andrews shook his head dolefully.

"I won't have this kind of nonsense in my facility. Do you all hear me? I will not put up with it." A faint scraping noise caused him to glance upward.

The alien reached down and nipped the superintendent off the floor as neatly as a spider trapping a fly. In an instant both predator and prey were gone. In the ensuing hysteria only Ripley and prisoner Morse actually saw the monster drag the quiescent form of Andrews into an open air shaft.

Ripley took up a seat in a corner and lit a narcostick. She found herself remembering Clemens. Her expression hardened. Clemens: better not to think of him, just as she'd learned to quickly forget several other men with whom she'd formed attachments, only to have them snatched away and destroyed by other representatives of the seemingly indestructive alien horde.

Except that they were not indestructible. They could be killed. And so long as she was alive, that seemed to be her destiny. To wipe them out, to eliminate them from the face of the universe. It was a calling she would gladly, oh, so gladly, have bequeathed to another.

Why her? It was a question she had pondered on more than one occasion. Why should she have been singled out? No, she reflected, that wasn't right. Nothing was singling her out. Fate hadn't chosen her to deal with a lifetime of horror and devastation. Others had confronted the aliens and perished. Only she continued to suffer because only she continued to survive.

It was a destiny she could abandon at any time. The infirmary was well stocked, its contents clearly labeled. A single, simple injection could wipe away all the pain and the terror. Easy enough to put an end to it. Except that she was a survivor. Perhaps that was her task in life, simply to survive. No, fate hadn't singled her out for special mistreatment. She wasn't responsible for the fact that she was tougher than anyone else. It was just something she'd have to learn to live with.

Another man gone. One she hadn't been especially fond of this time. She regretted it nonetheless. Andrews was human, and if nothing else deserved to die a decent death.

The alien had left dead silence in the wake of its astonishingly swift attack. In its aftermath the men had resumed sitting or standing, each staring into the distance, at his neighbor, or inwardly. As usual it was left to Dillon to kneel and begin the prayer.

"We have been given a sign, brothers. How we deal with it will determine our fates."

"Amen," several of the prisoners chorused. The comments of several others were fortunately unintelligible.

Dillon continued. "We give thanks, O Lord, your wrath has come and the time is near that we be judged. The apocalypse is upon us. Let us be ready. Let your mercy be just."

Near the back of the hall the prisoners had begun to whisper to one another, Dillon's prayer notwithstanding.

"It was big," prisoner David muttered. "I mean, *big*. And fast."

"I saw it, asshole." Kevin was gazing intently at the place on the ceiling from which the alien had hung. "I was there. Y'think I'm blind?"

"Yeah, but I mean it was big." So intent were they on the memory of what had just happened that they even forgot to stare at Ripley.

Prisoner William rose and surveyed his comrades. "Okay, so what do we do now, mates?" A couple of the men looked at one another but no one said anything. "Well, who's in charge? I mean, we need to get organized here, right?"

Aaron swallowed, glanced around the room. "I guess I'm next in line."

Morse rolled his eyes ceilingward. "Eighty-five's gonna be in charge. Jesus, give me a break!"

"Don't call me that!" Aaron glared at the prisoner who'd spoken. "Not now, not ever!" Rising, he advanced to confront them.

"Look, no way I can replace Andrews. I'm not even

gonna pretend that I can. You guys didn't appreciate him. I know he was a hardass sometimes, but he was the best man I ever worked with.''

Dillon was less than impressed. ''I don't want to hear that shit.'' His gaze shifted from the assistant to the lanky figure seated on the far side of the hall. ''What about you? You're an officer. How about showing us a little leadership?''

Ripley glanced briefly in his direction, took a puff on her narcostick, and looked away.

Williams broke the ensuing silence, gesturing at Dillon. ''You take over. You run things here anyway.''

The bigger man shook his head quickly. ''No fuckin' way. I ain't the command type. I just take care of my own.''

''Well, what's the fuckin' beast want?'' The discouraged Williams inquired aloud. ''Is the fucker gonna try and get us all?''

The narcostick eased from Ripley's lips. ''Yeah.''

''Well, isn't that sweet?'' Morse growled sarcastically. ''How do we stop it?''

Disgusted, Ripley tossed the remains of her narcostick aside and rose to confront the group.

''We don't have any weapons, right? No smart guns, no pulse rifles, nothing?''

Aaron nodded reluctantly. ''Right.''

She looked thoughtful. ''I haven't seen one exactly like this before. It's bigger, its legs are different. The other ones were afraid of fire, or at least respectful of it. Not much else.''

She let her gaze roam the hall. ''Can we seal off this area?''

''No chance,'' Aaron told her. ''The developed mine

complex is ten miles square. There's six hundred air ducts that access the surface. This goddamn place is big."

"What about video? We could try to locate it that way. I see monitors everywhere."

Again the assistant superintendent shook his head. "Internal video system hasn't worked in years. No reason to keep an expensive hi-tech system just to monitor a lousy twenty-five caretaker prisoners who aren't going anywhere anyhow. Fact is, nothin' much works here anymore. We got a lot of technology, but no way to fix it."

"What eight-five's tryin' to tell you—" Morse started to say.

"Don't call me that!" Aaron snapped.

The prisoner ignored him. "—is that we got no entertainment centers, no climate control, no viewscreens, no surveillance, no freezers, no fuckin' ice cream, no guns, no rubbers, no women. All we got here is shit."

"Shut up," Dillon said warningly.

"What the hell are we even talkin' to her for?" Morse continued. "She's the one that brought the fucker here. Let's run her head through the wall."

Ripley shrugged ever so slightly. "Sounds good to me."

Dillon walked over to confront Morse. "I won't say it again," he said softly. "Keep your mouth shut."

Morse considered, then dropped his gaze and backed off. For the time being.

The assistant super eyed Ripley. "All right. What do we do now?"

She was aware that not just the three men at the table but the majority of the prisoners were watching her, waiting.

"On Archeron we tried to seal ourselves off and

establish a defensive perimeter. It worked, but only for a little while. These things always find a way in. First I need to see, not hear, what our exact physical situation is.''

''It's fucked,'' Morse growled, but under his breath.

Aaron nodded. ''Come with me.'' He looked to Dillon. ''Sorry, but you know the regs.''

The big man blinked slowly by way of acknowledgment. ''Just don't be too long, okay?''

Aaron tried to grin, failed. ''Look at this way: no work detail today.''

Dillon let his gaze sweep the upper level of the library. ''Then why is it I don't feel relaxed?''

They moved along the main passageway, Aaron holding the schematic map, Ripley shifting her attention from the printout to the corridor and walls. There was overhead light, but dim. Morse was wrong. Some of the complex's basic life support system still functioned.

She tapped the plastic sheet. ''What's this?''

''Access serviceway. Connects the infirmary to the mess hall.''

''Maybe we can go in, flush it out.''

He stayed close. ''Come on. There's miles and miles of tunnels down there.''

She traced lines on the sheet. ''It won't go far. It'll nest in this area right around here, in one of the smaller passageways or air shafts.''

His expression twisted. ''Nest? Don't you mean 'rest'?''

She glanced over at him. ''I mean what I say. Just don't ask me for details. If we can kill or immobilize it, remind me and I'll explain. Otherwise you don't want to know.''

He held her stare a moment longer, then dropped his eyes back to the map. "How do you know that?"

"It's like a lion. It sticks close to the zebras."

"We don't have any zebras here."

She halted and gave him a look.

"Oh, right," he said, subdued. "But running around down there in the dark? You gotta be kiddin'. We got no overheads once you get out of the main shaft here."

"How about flashlights?"

"Sure. We got six thousand of them. And rechargeable batteries. But no bulbs. Somebody forgot that little detail. I told ya, nothin' works."

"What about torches? Do we have the capability of making fire? Most humans have enjoyed that privilege since the Stone Age."

The old vertical shaft stretched up and down into darkness, the ladder welded to its interior filthy with carboniferous grime and accumulated gunk. Damp air ascended languidly from the black depths, thick in Ripley's nostrils as she leaned out of the corridor and aimed her torch downward. No bottom was visible, not had she expected to see one.

They'd started in through the tunnel where Murphy had been killed, past the huge ventilator blades, which Aaron had shut down prior to their departure. She sniffed, wrinkled her nose. The rising air was more than damp; it was pungent with rotting vegetation and the sharp tang of recycled chemicals.

"What's down there?"

Aaron crowded close behind her. "Air and water purification and recirculation."

"Which explains the stink. Fusion?"

"Yeah, but sealed away. Everything operates on automatics. A couple of techs from the supply ship run a status check every six months." He grinned. "You don't think they'd trust the maintenance details of a functioning fusion plant to the delicate ministrations of a bunch of prisoners and a couple of prison administrators with general degrees, do you?"

She didn't smile back. "Nothing the Company does would surprise me." Holding on to the edge of the opening she aimed the torch upward, played the light over the smooth metal walls. "What's upstairs?"

"Low-tech stuff. Storage chambers, most of 'em empty now. Cleaned out when Weyland-Yutani closed down the mine. Service accessways. Power and water conduits. All the tunnels and shafts are bigger then they need to be. With all the drilling and coring equipment at hand the engineers were able to make it easy on themselves. They built everything oversized." He paused. "You think it might have gone up there somewhere?"

"It would naturally choose a large, comfortable chamber for a nest, and it likes to keep above its . . . prey. Drop down from above rather than come up from below. Also, the upper levels are closer to the prison habitat. That's where it'll expect us to be holed up. If we're lucky we might be able to come up behind it. If we're unlucky . . ."

"Yeah?" Aaron prompted.

"We might be able to come up behind it." She swung out onto the ladder and began climbing.

Not only was the ladder thick with encrusted grime, but the moist air rising from below had stimulated the growth of local algae and other microorganisms. The rungs were slippery and uneven. She made sure to grip the side of the ladder firmly with her free hand as she ascended.

The shaft intersected one of more cross-corridors approximately every three meters. At each level she shoved her torch inside, illuminating each tunnel for a respectable distance before resuming her ascent.

While he was trying to watch Ripley, Aaron's concentration slipped along with his foot. Behind him Dillon quickly looped his left arm around the ladder and caught the flailing ankle with his other hand, shoving the assistant super's boot back onto the nearest rung.

"You all right up there?" he inquired in a terse whisper.

"Fine," Aaron replied, albeit a little shakily. "Just keep that torch out of my ass."

"Funny you should mention that," the big man replied in the half darkness. "I've spent years dreaming of doing just that."

"Save it for another time, okay?" Aaron hurried himself, not wanting Ripley to get dangerously far ahead.

"One thing more, man," Dillon murmured.

The assistant superintendent glanced back down. "What now?"

"Anytime you want to trade places, you let me know."

"In your dreams." Despite their circumstances each man mustered a fraternal grin of understanding. Then they resumed climbing, the brief feeling of camaraderie swept away in the desperation and anxiety of their situation.

Ripley glanced down, wondering what they were talking about. It was good that they could manage to smile under such conditions. She wished she could share in their amusement, but knew she could not. She was much too conscious of what might lie ahead of them. Inhaling resignedly, she ascended the next step and aimed her light into still another opening.

Straight into the face of the creature.

If her fingers hadn't contracted in terror she surely would have fallen off the ladder as she screamed. Reflexively she swung her torch. It struck the horror square atop the gleaming black head . . . which crumbled into pieces on contact.

"What . . . what is it?" Aaron was yelling below her.

She ignored him as she fought to regain her equilibrium. Only then did she pull herself up the ladder and step off into the tunnel.

Together the three stared at the collapsed, dried-out husk of the adult alien.

"Ugly sucker, ain't it?" Dillon volunteered.

Ripley knelt to examine the cast-off shell. Her fingers trembled slightly as she touched it, then steadied. It was perfectly harmless, a shadow of an enigma. There was nothing there. The skull where her torch had struck had been empty inside. Experimentally she gave the remainder of the shell a light push and the massive, streamlined form tumbled over onto its side. She straightened.

"What is it?" Aaron asked her. He prodded the husk with his foot.

"It's shed its skin, molted somehow." She looked sharply up the tunnel. "This is a new one. I've never seen this before. Not at this stage of development."

"What's it mean?" Dillon muttered.

"Can't say. No precedent. One thing we can be sure of, though. It's bigger now."

"How much bigger?" Aaron joined her in peering up the dark passageway.

"That depends," Ripley murmured.

"On what?"

"On what it's become." She started forward, holding her light out in front of her as she pushed her way past him.

Something inside her urged her on, making her increase rather than slow the pace. She hardly paused long enough to shine her torch down the side passages that branched off the main tunnel. The discovery of the alien husk had charged her with the same sort of relentless determination that had enabled her to survive the devastation of Archeron. Determination, and a growing anger. She found herself thinking of Jonesy. No one wonder she and the cat had survived the *Nostromo*. Curiosity and a talent for survival were two of the skills they'd shared.

Jonesy was gone now, a victim of the time distortions made necessary by space travel. No more cat-nightmares for him. Only she was left to deal with life, and all the memories.

"Slow up." Aaron had to break into a jog to catch up with her. He held up the map, then gestured ahead. "Almost there."

She looked at him. "I hope this was worth the climb. What happened to all the damn lifts in this place?"

"You kidding? Deactivated when the installation was closed down. Why would a bunch of prisoners need to be in this sector anyway?" He started forward, taking the lead.

They walked another hundred meters before the tunnel opened up into a much larger passageway, one wide and high enough to accommodate vehicles as well as men. The assistant superintendent stopped next to the far wall, holding his torch out to illuminate a sign welded to the metal.

TOXIC WASTE STORAGE
THIS CHAMBER HERMETICALLY SECURED
NO ACCESS WITHOUT AUTHORIZATION
rating B-8 or Higher Required

"Well, well. What do we have here?" For the first time in days Ripley allowed herself to feel a twinge of hope.

"There's more than a dozen of these scattered around the facility." Aaron was bending to study the detailed inscription below the plate. "This is the closest one to our living quarters." He tapped the wall with his torch and sparks dribbled to the floor.

"They were gonna shove a lot of heavy-duty waste in here. Refining by-products, that sort of thing. Some of these are full and permanently sealed, others partially filled. Cheaper, easier, and safer than stuffing the junk into drums and dumping it out in space.

"This one's never been used. Maybe because it's so close to the habitat areas. Or maybe they just never got around to it, closed up shop before they needed the room. I've been inside. It's clean as a whistle in there."

Ripley studied the wall. "What's the access like?"

"Pretty much what you'd expect for a storage facility carrying this rating." He led her around to the front.

The door was scratched and filthy, but still impressive. She noted the almost invisible seams at the corners. "This is the only way in or out?"

Aaron nodded. "That's right. I checked the stats before we came down. Entrance is just big enough for a small loader-transporter with driver and cargo. Ceiling, walls, and floor are six feet thick, solid ceramocarbide steel. So's the door. All controls and active components are external, or embedded in the matrix itself."

"Let's make sure we've got this right. You get something in there and close the door, no way it can get out?"

Aaron grunted confidently. "Right. No fuckin' way. That sucker is tight. According to the specs it'll hold a perfect vacuum. Nothin' bigger than a neutrino could slip through. That ceramocarbide stuff even dissipates lasers. You'd need a controlled nuclear explosion to cut your way in.''

"You sure this thing is still operational?"

He indicated a nearby control box. "Why don't you find out?"

She moved forward and broke the thin seal that covered the enclosure. The lid flipped down, exposing several controls. She studied them for a moment, then thumbed a large green button.

The immense door didn't so much slide aside as appear to vanish silently into the wall. She cycled it again, admiring the smooth play of forces that could shift so much mass with such speed and ease. The prisoners were similarly impressed. The efficiency of the long-dormant technology lifted their spirits considerably.

Beyond the open barrier was a slick-walled, empty chamber. An ephemeral coating of dust covered the floor. It would accommodate several full-grown aliens with ease.

"Let me see the map." Aaron handed her the sheet and her index finger drew patterns on the plastic. "We're here?" He leaned close and nodded. "Administration's here, assembly hall up this corridor?"

"You got it. Fast, too," he added admiringly.

"I owe the fact that I'm still alive to an understanding of spatial relationships." She tapped the sheet. "If we can get it to chase us down these passageways, here and here, then close these off one at a time, we might get it inside." The three of them stared into the storage chamber.

Dillon looked back at her. "Lemme get this straight. You wanna burn it down and outta the pipes, force it here, slam the door, and trap its ass?"

She spoke without looking up from the map. "Ummm."

"And you're looking for help from us Y-chromo boys."

"You got something better to do?"

"Why should we put our asses on the line for you?"

She finally glanced up at him, her eyes steely. "Your asses are already on the line. The only question is what you're going to do about it."

- X -

Accompanied by prisoner David, Aaron showed Ripley through the vast storage chamber. When they reached the section where the drums were stored, he paused and pointed.

"This is where we keep it. I don't know what this shit's called."

"Quinitricetyline," David supplied helpfully.

"I knew that," the assistant superintendent grumbled as he checked his notepad. "Okay. I'm off to work out the section assignments with Dillon for the paintbrush team. David, you get these drums organized, ready to move." He turned and headed in the direction of the main corridor.

"Right, Eight-five," David called after him.

"Don't call me that!" Aaron vanished into the darkness of the distant corridor.

Ripley examined the drums. They were slightly corroded and obviously hadn't been touched in some time, but otherwise appeared intact.

"What's this 'Eight-five' thing?"

David put gloved hands on the nearest container. "Lot of the prisoners used to call him that. We got his personnel charts out of the computer a few years ago. It's his IQ." He grinned as he started to roll the drum.

Ripley stood and watched. "He seems to have a lot of faith in this stuff. What's your opinion?"

The prisoner positioned the drum for loading. "Hell, I'm just a dumb watchman, like the rest of the guys here. But I did see a drum of this crap fall into a beachhead bunker once. Blast put a tug in dry dock for seventeen weeks. Great stuff."

In another part of the storage chamber prisoners Troy and Arthur sorted through the mass of discarded electronics components. Troy shoved a glass bead into the cylinder he was holding, thumbed the switch, then disgustedly wrenched the bead free and began hunting for another.

"Goddamn it. One fucking bulb in two thousand works."

His companion looked up from his own search. "Hey, it could be a lot worse. We mighta got the paintbrush detail." He tried a bead in his own tube, hit the switch. To his astonishment and delight, it lit.

The two men filled the air duct with little room to spare, slathering the interior surface with the pungent quinitricetyline.

"This shit smells awful," Prisoner Kevin announced for the hundredth time. His companion barely deigned to reply.

"I've told you already; don't breathe it."

"Why not?"

"Fuckin' fumes."

"I'm in a fuckin' pipe with it. How can I keep from breathing it?"

Outside the toxic waste storage chamber other men were dumping buckets of the QTC and spreading it around as best they could, with brooms and mops and, where those were lacking, with their booted feet.

In the corridor Dillon was waiting with Ripley. Everything was proceeding according to plan, though whether the plan would proceed according to plan remained to be seen.

He glanced toward her, analyzed the expression on her face. Not that he was particularly sensitive, but he'd seen a lot of life.

"You miss the doc, right?"

"I didn't know him very well," she muttered by way of reply.

"I thought you two got real close."

Now she looked over at him. "I guess you've been looking through some keyholes."

Dillon smiled. "That's what I thought."

The nausea didn't slip up on her; it attacked hard and fast, overwhelming her equilibrium, forcing her to lean against the wall for support as she gagged and coughed. Dillon moved to support her but she shoved him away, fighting for air. He eyed her with sudden concern.

"You okay?"

She took a deep breath and nodded.

"Whatever you say. But you don't look okay to me, sister."

*   *   *

Aaron surveyed the convicts who'd accompanied him—some nearby, others on the walkway above. All carried primed emergency flares which would ignite on hard contact.

"Okay, listen up." All eyes turned to regard him attentively. "Don't light this fire till I give you the signal. This is the signal." He raised his arm. "You guys got it? Think you can remember that?"

They were all intent on him. So intent that the man nearest the vertical air duct dropped the flare he'd been holding. He clutched at it, missed, and held his breath as it slid to the ledge near his feet.

His companion hadn't noticed. Straining, he knelt to retrieve it, let out a sigh of relief . . .

As the alien appeared behind the grate on which the flare lay poised precariously, and reached for him.

The man managed to scream, the flare flipping from his fingers to fall to the ground below.

Where it flowered brightly.

Aaron heard and saw the explosion simultaneously. His eyes widened. "No, goddamn it! Wait for the fucking signal! Shit!"

Then he saw the alien and forgot about the flames.

They spread as rapidly as the desperate planners had hoped, shooting down QTC-painted corridors, licking up air vents, frying soaked floors and walkways. In her own corridor Ripley heard the approaching flames and pressed herself against unpainted ground as the air vents overhead caught. A convict nearby wasn't as fast. He screamed as heat ignited his clothing.

Morse rolled wildly away from the licking flames, in time to see the alien scuttle past overhead.

"It's over here! Hey, it's here!" No one had the inclination or ability to respond to his alarm.

It was impossible to keep track of half of what was happening. Injured men flung themselves from burning railings or dropped from the hot ceiling. Prisoner Eric saw the fire reaching for him and darted at the last possible instant into the safety of an uncoated service pipe, barely squeezing through in time to avoid the blast of fire that seared the bottoms of his feet. Another man died as the alien emerged from a steaming ventilation duct to land directly on him.

Running like mad, Aaron and one of the convicts raced for the waste disposal chamber, trying to stay ahead of the flames. The assistant superintendent made it; his companion wasn't quite as fast . . . or as lucky. The fire engulfed but did not stop him.

As they stumbled into the storage chamber junction, Ripley, Dillon, and prisoner Junior managed to knock the burning man to the floor and beat at the flames on his back. Aaron fought to catch his breath. As he did so a scuttling sound overhead caught his attention. With unexpected presence of mind he grabbed a QTC-soaked mop and jabbed it into the nearby flames. Holding the makeshift torch aloft, he jammed it into the gaping overhead duct port. The scuttling noise faded.

The prisoner died in Junior's arms, his mouth working without producing words. Junior rose and charged into the smoke and fire, screaming.

"Come and get me, chino! Come and get me!"

In the main access corridor smoke inhalation toppled another man. The last thing he saw as he went down was the alien rising before him, silhouetted by the flames and the incredible heat. He tried to scream too, but failed.

Junior turned a corner and skidded to a halt. As he did so the alien whirled.

"Run, run!" The grieving prisoner charged past the monster, which gave chase without hesitation.

They all converged near the entrance to the toxic storage facility; Ripley and Dillon, Aaron and Morse, the other surviving prisoners. As the alien turned to confront them they emulated Aaron's example, lighting mops and heaving the makeshift missiles at the beast. Junior took the opportunity to move up close behind it.

"Here! Take a shot, fucker!"

Where quarry was concerned the alien once again demonstrated its inclination to choose proximity over proliferation. Whirling, it pounced on Junior. The two tumbled backward . . . into the storage chamber.

Struggling to ward of the intense heat, Dillon continued to extinguish flaming companions. When the last man was merely smoldering, he turned and tried to penetrate the flames to reach the back wall.

Ripley reached the control box and fumbled for the red button as Aaron jammed still another flaming mop into the entrance. A moment later Dillon managed to activate the sprinkler system.

Junior uttered a last, faint, hopeless cry as the heavy door slammed shut in front of him, sealing off the storage chamber. At the same time the showers opened up. Exhausted, terrified men, all with varying degrees of smoke or burn damage, hovered motionless in the corridor as the water poured down.

A noise from behind the door then, a distant skittering sound. Things that were not hands exploring, not-fingers scraping at their surroundings. The trapped alien was hunting, searching, for a way out. Gradually the noise ceased.

A couple of the survivors looked at one another as if about to burst into cheers. Ripley anticipated them curtly.

"It's not over."

One of the men retorted angrily, "Bullshit. It's inside, the door worked. We've got it."

"What are you talking about?" Aaron challenged her. "We got the bastard trapped, just like you planned it."

Ripley didn't even look at him. She didn't have to explain herself because the silence was suddenly rocked by an ear-splitting concussion. A few of the men winced and a couple turned to run.

The rest gaped in amazement at the door, in which a huge convex dent had suddenly appeared. The echo of contact continued to cannonade along the multiple corridors. Before it had faded entirely a second thunderous boom reverberated through the antechamber and a second bulge appeared in the door.

"Son of a bitch," Aaron muttered aloud, "that's a ceramocarbide door."

Dillon wasn't listening to him. A survivor of another kind, he was watching Ripley. She hadn't moved, so neither did he. If she started running he'd follow close on her heels, without any intention of stopping.

But she continued to hold her ground as a third dent manifested itself. His ears rang. *This is a lady I wish I'd known before,* he mused silently. *A lady who could change a man, alter the course and direction of his life. She could have changed mine. But that was before. Too late now. Been too late for a long time.*

No more concussive vibrations rattled his eardrums. No fourth bulge appeared in the barrier. Dead silence ruled the corridor. Gradually everyone's attention shifted from that no longer perfect but still intact doorway back to the single woman in their midst.

When she slowly sat down and closed her eyes, back against one wall, the unified sigh of relief that filled the room was like the last failing breeze that marks the passing of a recent storm.

· XI ·

The survivors gathered in the assembly hall, reduced in number but expanded in spirit. Dillon stood before them, waiting to make sure all were present. Only then did he begin.

"Rejoice, brothers! Even for those who have fallen this is a time of rejoicing. Even as we mourn their passing we salute their courage. Because of their sacrifice, we live, and who is to say which of us, the living or the dead, has the better deal?

"Of one thing we are certain: they have their reward. They are in a far better place because there can be no worse one. They will live forever. Rejoice. Those who are dead but go on, freed of their restraints, free from the excoriations of a thoughtless society. It abandoned them, and now they have abandoned it. They have moved up. They have moved higher. Rejoice and give thanks!"

The men bowed their heads and began to murmur softly to themselves.

Ripley and Aaron watched from the gallery above. Eventually the assistant superintendent glanced over at his companion. Both had spent time in the showers. They were far from refreshed, but at least they were clean. Ripley had delighted in the hot, pounding spray, knowing that this time she could enjoy it without having to keep a wary eye on the sealtight or the vents.

"What do you think of this?" He indicated the ragged, makeshift assemblage below.

She'd been listening with only half a mind, the rest of her thoughts elsewhere. "Not much. I guess if they take pleasure in it . . ."

"You got it right there. Fuckers are crazy. But it keeps 'em quiet. The super and I were in agreement on that. Andrews always said it was a good thing Dillon and his meatballs were hung up on this holy roller crap. Makes 'em more docile."

She glanced back at him. "You're not the religious type."

"Me? Shit, no. I got a job." He looked thoughtful. "I figure rescue team gets here in four, five days. Six, tops. They open the door, go in there with smart guns, and kill the bastard. Right?"

"Have you heard anything from them?" Her tone was noncommittal.

"Naw." He was feeling pretty good about the situation. And about himself. Out of this mess there was sure to come some good things.

"We only got a 'message received.' No details. Later we got something that said you were top priority. Again, no explanation. They don't cut us in on much. We're the ass-end of the totem pole out here."

"Look," she began guardedly, "if the Company wants to take the thing back—"

"Take it back? Are you kiddin'? They aren't lunatics, you know. They'll kill it right away." He frowned at her, then shrugged mentally. Sometimes he thought he understood this unusual woman perfectly, and then she'd throw him a complete curve.

Well, it wasn't his business to understand her; only to keep her alive. That was what Weyland-Yutani wanted. With Andrews gone and the alien safely contained, he was beginning to see some possibilities in the situation. Not only was he now the one in charge, it would be up to him to greet and explain things to the Company representative. He could render himself, as well as recent events, memorable in the eyes of his superiors. There might be a bonus in it for him or, even better, early retirement from Fiorina. It was not too much to hope for.

Besides, after years of toadying to Andrews and after what he'd been through the past couple of days, he'd earned whatever came his way.

"Hey, you're really concerned about this, aren't you? Why? What's there to be worried about? The damn thing's locked up where it can't get at us."

"It's not the alien. It's the Company. I've gone around with them on this twice before." She turned to him. "They've coveted one of these things ever since my original crewmates discovered them. For bioweapons research. They don't understand what they're dealing with, and I don't care how much data they've accumulated on it. I'm concerned that they might want to try and take this one back."

He gaped at her, and she found his honest disbelief

reassuring. For the moment, at least, she was not without allies.

"Take it back? You mean alive? To Earth?"

She nodded.

"You've got to be kidding."

"Look into my eyes, Aaron. This isn't a real humorous subject with me."

"Shit, you mean it. That's insane. They gotta kill it."

Ripley smiled tightly. "Right. So I take it that we're agreed on this point?"

"You're damn right," he said fervently.

He was with her, then, she mused. For now. The Company had a way of swaying people, inducing them to reassess their positions. Not to mention their values.

The infirmary was quiet. Peace had returned to the installation, if not to some of its inhabitants. Concerned that in Clemens's absence certain of the prisoners whose presence on Fiorina stemmed at least in part from their personal misapplication of certain proscribed pharmaceuticals might attempt to liberate them or their chemical cousins from their designated repository, Aaron sent Morse to keep an eye on them, as well as on the infirmary's sole occupant.

Morse sat on one of the cots, perusing a viewer. He was not one of those despondent over the dearth of entertainment material available on Fiorina, since he'd never been much of one for casual diversions. He was a man of action, or had been in his younger, more active days. Now he was a spieler, dealing in reminiscences.

Despite the fact that they'd known each other and had worked side by side for years, Golic had offered no greeting at his arrival, nor a single word since. Now the hulking prisoner finally turned his face away from the wall, his arms still buried inside the archaic restraining jacket.

"Hey, Morse."

The older man looked up from his viewer. "So you can still talk. Big deal. You never had nothin' to say anyhow."

"C'mon, brother. Let me out of this thing."

Morse grinned unpleasantly. "Oh, so now that you're all wrapped up like a holiday roast suddenly I'm a 'brother'? Don't give me any shit."

"Come on, man. Don't be like that. This thing's uncomfortable as hell. Gimmie a break."

"No fucking way. I got my orders."

"C'mon, man, it hurts."

"Sorry." Morse turned back to his viewer. "Aaron says to let you go, I'll let you go. Until then you stay tied up. I don't wanna get in no trouble. Not with a Company ship coming."

"I didn't do nothing. I mean, I understand I was a little crazy for a while. Shit, who wouldn't be after what I saw? But I'm okay now. The doc fixed me. Just ask him."

"Can't do that. The doc bought it. You heard."

"Oh, yeah. That's right. I remember now. Too bad. He was a good guy, even if he did slap me in this."

"Don't talk to me." Morse made a disgusted face.

Golic continued to plead. "What'd I do? Just tell me, what'd I do?"

Morse sighed and set the viewer aside, eying his fellow prisoner. "I dunno, but I'll tell you what I'm going to do. I'm gonna guard your ass just like I was ordered."

Golic sniffed derisively. "You afraid of that pissant Aaron?"

"No, I ain't, even if he is the unofficial superintendent

now. I just don't want no trouble with Dillon, and if you're smart, which I doubt, neither do you.''

The bigger man sniffed glumly. "All I did was tell about the dragon. About what it did to Boggs and Rains. Nobody believed me, but I wasn't lying. I should be the last one to be tied up. It ain't fair. You know what I'm sayin' is true. You saw it.''

Morse remembered. "Fuckin'-A I saw it! It was big. And fast. Man, it was fast. And ug-ly." He shuddered slightly. "There's cleaner ways to die.''

"Hey, that's right.'' Golic struggled futilely against his restraints. "Let me loose, man. You got to let me loose. What if it gets in here? I couldn't even run. I'd be dead meat.''

"You'd be dead meat anyway. I saw enough to know that. But it doesn't matter because it ain't gonna get in here.'' He smiled proudly. "We got it trapped. Me and the others. Locked up tight. I'll bet it's good and mad. The Company'll deal with it when the ship gets here.''

"That's right,'' Golic agreed readily. "And the way I hear it, they'll be here soon. So what's the big deal? Why should I have to hang around like this? By the time the ship shows orbit my arms'll be dead. I'll need surgery, and all for nothin'. Come on, man. You know they ain't gonna take me offworld for no surgery, and we may not get a new medic for months. I'll have to suffer all that time, and it'll all be your fault.''

"Hey, lay off. I didn't put you in that.''

"No, but you're keepin' me in it, and the guy that gave the order's dead now. Aaron doesn't give a shit. He's too busy trying to make that lady lieutenant. Has he even asked about me?''

"Well, no,'' Morse admitted guardedly.

"See?" Golic's face was full of pathetic eagerness. "I won't cause you no trouble, Morse. I'll lay low until the ship gets here. Aaron won't even know I'm around. Come on, lemme loose. I'm hungry. What's the big deal? Didn't I always give you free ciggies before anybody else?"

"Well . . . yeah."

"You're my friend. I love you."

"Yeah, I love you too." Morse hesitated, then cursed softly. "Fuck it, why not? Nobody deserves to be tied up like an animal all day. Not even a big dumb schmuck like you. But you're gonna behave yourself. No fuckin' around or I'll get nothin' but shit."

"Sure, Morse. Anything you say." He turned to present his back and Morse began undoing the seals on the straps. "No problem. Trust me, buddy. I'd do it for you."

"Yeah, but I ain't crazy enough to get myself in a sack like this. They know I'm sane," the other man said.

"C'mon, don't make fun of me. Do I sound like I'm crazy? 'Course not. It's just that everybody likes to make fun of me because I like to eat all the time."

"It's not that you like to eat, it's your table manners, man." Morse guffawed at his own humor as he undid the strap. "That's got it."

"Gimmie a hand, willya? My arms are so numb I can't move 'em."

"Shit. Bad enough they ask me to keep an eye on you, now I gotta play nursemaid too." He reached up and pulled the jacket off Golic. The bigger man helped as best he could.

"Where they got it?"

"Up in the nearest waste tank on Level Five. Man, did we get that sucker nailed down! I mean tight." He fairly preened. "Fuckin' marines couldn't do it, but we did."

Golic was swinging his arms. Back and forth across his expansive chest, then up and around in ever-widening circles, getting the circulation back.

"But it's still alive?"

"Yeah. Too bad. You oughta see the dents it put in the door. Ceramocarbide door, man!" He shook his head wonderingly. "One tough-ass organism. But we got it."

"I gotta see it again." The big man's gaze was focused on a point beyond Morse, on something visible only to Golic. His expression was impassive, unwavering. "Got to see it again. He's my friend."

Morse took a sudden, wary step backward. "What the fuck you talkin' about?" His gaze whipped to the infirmary entrance.

Golic calmly ripped a small fire extinguisher off the nearby wall and the other man's eyes widened. He made a leap for the door . . . too slow. The extinguisher came down once, a second time, and Morse crumpled like a misplaced intention.

Golic looked down at him thoughtfully, his face full of idiot sadness, his tone apologetic. "Sorry, brother, but I had a feeling you wouldn't understand. No more ciggies for you, mate."

Silently he stepped over the unconscious form and exited the room.

- XII -

Aaron fussed with the deep-space communicator. He was checked out on the equipment—it was a requirement of his rating—but he hadn't had occasion to make use of it since his assignment to Fiorina. Andrews had always handled things on the rare occasions when expensive near instantaneous communication between the installation and headquarters had been required. He was both pleased and relieved when the readouts cleared for use, indicating that contact with the necessary relays had been established.

Ripley hovered over him as he worked the keyboard. She offered no suggestions, for which he felt an obscure but nonetheless real gratitude. The message appeared on the main screen as he transmitted, each letter representing an impressive amount of sending power. Fortunately, with the fusion plant operating as efficiently as ever, there was no dearth of the necessary energy. As to the cost, another matter entirely, he opted to ignore that until and unless the Company should indicate otherwise.

FURY 361—CLASS C PRISON UNIT, FIORINA

REPORT DEATH OF SUPT. ANDREWS, MEDICAL OFFICER CLEMENS, EIGHT PRISONERS. NAMES TO FOLLOW . . .

When he'd finished the list he glanced back up at her. "Okay, we got the first part. All nice and formal, the way the Company likes it. Now what do I say?"

"Tell them what happened. That the alien arrived on the EEV and escaped into the complex, that it was hunting down the local population one man at a time until we devised a plan of action, and that we've trapped it."

"Right." He turned back to the keyboard, hesitated. "What do we call it? Just 'the alien'?"

"That'd probably do for the Company. They'd know what you were referring to. Technically it's a xenomorph."

"Right." He hesitated. "How do you spell it?"

"Here." She elbowed him aside impatiently and leaned over the keyboard. "With your permission?"

"Go ahead," he said expansively. Impressed, he watched as her fingers flew over the keys.

HAVE TRAPPED XENOMORPH. REQUEST PERMISSION TO TERMINATE.

Aaron frowned up at her as she stood back from the board. "That was a waste. We can't kill it. We don't have any weapons here, remember?"

Ripley ignored him, concentrating on the lambent screen. "We don't have to tell them that."

"Then why ask?" He was obviously confused, and she was in no hurry to enlighten him. Just then there were more important things on her mind.

Sure enough, letters began to appear on the readout.

She smiled humorlessly. They weren't wasting any time replying, no doubt for fear that in the absence of a ready response she might simply proceed.

TO FURY 361—CLASS C PRISON UNIT
FROM NETWORK COMCON WEYLAND-YUTANI
MESSAGE RECEIVED

Aaron leaned back in the chair and rubbed his forehead tiredly. "See? That's all they ever tell us. Treat us like shit, like we're not worth the expense of sending a few extra words."

"Wait," she told him.

He blinked. Subsequent to the expected official acknowledgment, letters continued to appear on the screen.

RESCUE UNIT TO ARRIVE YOUR ORBIT 1200 HOURS. STAND BY TO RECEIVE. PERMISSION DENIED TO TERMINATE XENOMORPH. AVOID CONTACT UNTIL RESCUE TEAM ARRIVES. REPEAT IMPERATIVE—PERMISSION DENIED.

There was more, in the same vein, but Ripley had seen enough. "Shit." She turned away, chewing her lower lip thoughtfully. "I knew it."

Aaron's gaze narrowed as he tried to divide his attention between Ripley and the screen. "What do you mean, you knew it? It doesn't mean anything. They know we don't have any weapons."

"Then why the 'imperative'? Why the anxious insistence that we don't do something they must realize we're not capable of doing?"

He shrugged uncomprehendingly. "I guess they don't want to take any chances."

"That's right," she murmured tightly. "They don't want to take any chances."

"Hey," he said, suddenly alarmed, "you're not thinking of countermanding Company policy, are you?"

Now she did smile. "Who me? Perish the thought."

The vestibule outside the toxic storage chamber was
dimly illuminated, but he inadequate light did not trouble
the three prisoners on duty. There was nothing in the shafts
and tunnels that could harm them, and no noise from
within. The three dents stood out clearly in the heavy door.
They had not been expanded, nor had they been joined by a
fourth.

One man leaned casually against the wall, cleaning
the dirt from under his nails with a thin sliver of plastic.
His companion sat on the hard, cold floor, conversing
softly.

"And I say the thing's gotta be dead by now." The
speaker had sandy hair flecked with gray at the temples and
a large, curving nose that in another age and time would
have given him the aspect of a Lebanese merchant.

"How you figure that?" the other man asked.

"You heard the boss. Nothin' can get in or out of that
box." He jerked a thumb in the direction of the storage
chamber. "Not even gases."

"Yeah. So?"

The first man tapped the side of his head with a finger.
"Think, stupid. If gas can't get out, that means air can't get
in. That sucker's been in there long enough already to use
up all the air twice over."

The other glanced at the dented door. "Well, maybe."

"What d'you mean, maybe? It's big. That means it
uses a lot of air. A lot more than a human."

"We don't know that." His companion wore the somber air of the unconvinced. "It ain't human. Maybe it uses less air. Or maybe it can hibernate or somethin'."

"Maybe you oughta go in and check on how it's doin'." The nail-cleaner looked up from his work with a bored expression. "Hey, did you hear something?"

The other man suddenly looked to his right, into the dim light of the main tunnel.

"What's the matter?" His companion was grinning. "The boogeyman out there?"

"No, dammit, I heard something." Footsteps then, clear and coming closer.

"Shit." The nail-cleaner moved away from the wall, staring.

A figure hove into view, hands clasped behind its back. The two men relaxed. There was some uneasy laughter.

"Dammit, Golic." The man resumed his seat on the floor. "You might've let us know it was you. Whistled or something."

"Yeah," said his companion. He waved at the chamber. "I don't think it can whistle."

"I'll remember," the big man told them. His expression was distant and he swayed slightly from side to side.

"Hey, you okay, man? You look weird," said the nail-cleaner.

His companion chuckled. "He always looks weird."

"It's okay," Golic muttered. "Let's go. Off and on. I gotta get in there." He nodded toward the chamber.

The two men on the floor exchanged a puzzled glance, one carefully slipping his nail cleaner into a pocket. He was watching the new arrival closely.

"What the hell's he talkin' about?" the theory-spinner wondered.

"Fucker's crazy," his companion declared with conviction.

"What you want here, man? When did they let you out of the infirmary, anyway?"

"It's all right." Golic's face shone with beatific determination. "I just need to go in there and see the Beast. We got a lot of shit to talk over." he added, as if that explained everything. "I gotta go in there. You understand."

"No, I don't understand. But I do know one thing. Neither you nor anyone else is goin' in there, dickhead. Big motherfucker'd eat you alive. Plus, you let that fucker out, and you can kiss our collective ass good-bye. Don't you know nothin', brother?"

"You wanna commit suicide," declared his companion, "go jump down a mine shaft. But you're not doin' it here. The super'd have our butts." He started toward the intruder.

"The Superintendent is dead," Golic announced solemnly as he brought out the club he'd been holding behind his back and used it to mash the skull of the man coming toward him.

"What the fuck? . . . Get him—!"

Golic was much faster and far more agile than they imagined, but then this time he was driven by something a good deal more powerful than a simple lust for food. The two men went down beneath the club, their heads and faces bloodied. It was all over very quickly. Golic didn't pause to see if his companions were still alive because he didn't really care. All that mattered to him now was the obsession which had taken complete control of his mind, his emotions, his very being.

He regarded the two bodies sprawled at his feet. "I didn't really want to do that. I'll talk to your mothers. I'll explain it."

Dropping the club, he walked up to the door and ran his fingers over the dented alloy. Pressing one ear to the smooth surface, he listened intently. No sound, no scraping, nothing. He giggled softly and moved to the control box, studying it thoughtfully for a long moment, much as a child would examine a complex new toy.

Chuckling to himself, he began fiddling with the controls, running his fingers playfully over the buttons until one clicked home. Deep within the surrounding ceramocarbide, mechanisms whined, metal brushed against metal. The door started to slide aside.

Only to halt as one of the big dents banged up against the jamb.

Frowning, Golic put his body into the narrow gap and pushed against the reluctant barrier, straining with his bulk. Motors hummed in confusion. The door opened a little wider, then stopped completely. The whir of the motor died. Silence reigned once more.

His body blocking the opening, Golic turned to peer into the blackness within. "Okay, I'm here. It's done. Just tell me what you want. Just tell me what to do, brother." He smiled.

The darkness ahead was silent as a tomb. Nothing moved within.

"Let's get this straight. I'm with you all the way. I just want to do my job. You just gotta tell me what to do next."

Though it lingered in the still air for quite some time, the two unconscious, bleeding men sprawled on the floor did not hear the singular high-pitched scream.

* * *

Dillon relaxed on his cot, engaged in his thousandth or ten thousandth game of solitaire. Idly he turned over another card and fingered his one long dreadlock as he spoke to the woman who stood before him.

"You're tellin' me they're comin' to take this thing away?"

"They'll try," Ripley assured him. "They don't want to kill it."

"Why? It don't make no sense."

"I agree completely, but they'll try anyway. I've gone around with them on this before. They look on the alien as a potential source of new bioproducts, perhaps even a weapons system."

Dillon chuckled, a deep, rich sound. But he was clearly disturbed at the idea. "Man, they're crazy."

"They won't listen. They think they know everything. That because nothing on Earth can touch them, this thing can't either. But it doesn't care how much power, how many politicians the Company controls. They try to take it back for study and it'll take over. The risk is too great. We've got to figure out some way to finish it off before they get here."

"From what you're tellin' me they ain't gonna like that much."

"I don't give a damn what they think. I know better than anyone, better than any of their so-called specialists, what these things can do. Sure you can build a cell that'll hold one. We've proven that here. But these things are patient. And they'll exploit the slimmest opportunity. Make one slip with them and it's all over. That doesn't mean a lot here, or on an isolated little outcolony like Archeron. But if these things ever get loose on Earth, it'll make Armageddon seem like a school picnic.''

The big man fingered his dreadlock as he puffed away on his relaxer. ''Sister, I lost a lot of the faithful trappin' the motherfucker. Men I'd known and lived with for some long, hard years. There weren't many of us here to begin with and I'm gonna to miss them.'' He looked up. ''Me and my brothers ain't gonna be the ones goin' in there and hittin' it with a stick.

''Why do we have to kill it anyway, if the Company's coming for it? Let them worry about it.''

She held her temper. ''I told you. They're going to try to take it back to Earth.''

He shrugged indifferently. ''What's wrong with that?''

''It'll destroy them. They can't control it. I told you, it'll kill them all. Everyone.''

He lay on his back, eying the ceiling and puffing contentedly. ''Like I said, what's wrong with that?''

Footsteps came pounding down the corridor outside the big man's room. He sat up curiously as Ripley turned.

Morse halted, breathing hard. His gaze darted from one to the other. Clearly he hadn't expected to find Ripley there. 'Hey, Dillon!''

The big man removed the smoker from his lips. ''You're interrupting a private discussion, brother.''

Morse glanced anew at Ripley, then back to his fellow prisoner. ''Put it on hold. I think we got a very large fucking problem, mate.''

Aaron was no medical tech, but it didn't take a doctor to see how the two men had been killed. Their heads had been bashed in. That wasn't the alien's technique. The bloody club lying nearby only confirmed his suspicions. As for the one who'd killed them, he hadn't profited by his deed. Golic's mutilated corpse lay nearby.

Aaron rose to join the others in gazing numbly at the gap in the toxic storage chamber's doorway. Dillon had stuck a torch inside, confirmed that it was empty.

"This cuts it," the acting superintendent muttered angrily. "Miserable son of a bitch let it loose. Crazy fucker. Got what he deserved, by God. Now what the fuck are we gonna do? Andrews was right. We should've kept the dumb shithead chained up or sedated. Stupid-ass rehab 'experts'." He paused, eying Ripley with some concern. "What's the matter? Side effects again?"

She was leaning against the wall for support, sucking air in long, awkward gasps and holding her stomach with her other hand.

"Piss on her," Morse growled. "The fuckin' thing's loose out there." He looked around wildly. "Now what the fuck are we gonna do?"

"I just said that," Aaron growled. "You're the dumb prick that let Golic go. You miserable little shit, you've killed all of us!"

For a man of undistinguished physique he packed an impressive punch. Morse went down hard, blood streaming from his nose. As the acting superintendent loomed over him he was grabbed from behind. Dillon easily lifted him off the floor and set him aside. Aaron glared back at the big man, panting.

"Cut that shit out," Dillon warned him.

"Watch yourself, Dillon! I'm still in charge here."

"I ain't disputing it. But you don't be doin' that. You get me? You don't be beating on the brothers. That's my job."

They regarded each other a moment longer. Then

Aaron took a deep breath and looked away, back down at the cringing Morse. "Then tell your fuckin' bozo to shape up. All this shit is his fault!"

Dillon ignored both of them as he turned to Ripley. "What do you think? We took care of it once. We still got a chance?"

She was still leaning against the wall, breathing hard, her expression twisted. Her head was killing her. When she finally looked up her face was knotted with pain and nausea.

"I need . . . I need to get to the EEV."

"Yeah, sure, but first we got to decide what to do about the creature."

"No." She shook her head sharply, her eyes watering slightly. "EEV first . . . now."

Aaron watched her anxiously. "Yeah, okay. No problem. Whatever you say. But why?"

"The neuroscanner. I need to use one of the scanners that are built into every cryotube. I don't know if you've got anything similar in the infirmary but it wouldn't matter if you did. Clemens is gone, and I only know how to operate the instrumentation on the EEV. If it's still functional." She winced, bending forward and clutching at her belly.

Dillon took a step toward her, beating Aaron to her side. This time she didn't object to the hands that helped steady her. She leaned against the big man for support until her breathing slowed.

"What the hell's wrong with you? You don't look so good."

"Side effects from medication Clemens was giving her," Aaron told him. His gaze narrowed uncertainly. "I think."

"Who gives a shit what's wrong with her?" Morse snapped. "What are *we* gonna do?"

Aaron glared at him. "You want to hit your back again, you little dork? Shut the fuck up and quit causin' panic."

Morse didn't back off. "Panic! You're so goddam dumb, you couldn't spell it. Don't tell me about panic! We ought to panic! We're screwed!"

"Yeah! And who's fault is it?"

"Both of you, shut up!" Dillon roared.

For a moment there was silence as each man glared at his neighbor but did not speak. Eventually Aaron shrugged.

"Okay, I'm out of ideas. What do we do?"

"What about the beach?" Morse opined hopefully.

"Right," the acting superintendent responded sarcastically. "The sun won't be up for another week, and when it's down it's forty below zero outside. The rescue team is ten hours away, so that makes a lot of sense."

"Wonderful," Morse grumbled as Ripley turned and wandered off. "So you just want us to stay here and let this fuckin' beast eat us for lunch."

"Get everybody that's still left together," Dillon told him abruptly. "Get 'em to the assembly hall. Lieutenant, you can—" He looked around, puzzled. "Where'd she go?"

Within the vast unloading bay the Emergency Escape Vehicle rested where it had been left, undisturbed and looking lonely in the flickering industrial gloom. Footsteps echoed along walkways, precise and finite in the metal-walled pit. Faint illumination preceded feet, lighting the way through the semi-darkness.

Ripley stripped down in the cramped quarters, carefully

setting her clothes aside. Naked, she sat down opposite a small keyboard. Several attempts were required before it flickered to life.

Her fingers worked the keyboard. She paused, played the keys again, then sat staring thoughtfully at the information displayed on the small screen. Rising, she left the readout and turned to the cryotube that had conveyed her to Fiorina.

It was an effort to squeeze back inside, and when she turned to work on the keyboard her hand barely reached.

"You need some help?"

She stared at Aaron's sudden appearance.

"Hey, didn't mean to scare you. Look, you shouldn't be wandering around alone."

"I've heard that one before. Do me a favor. Run the keyboard. I can't reach over and see what I'm doing."

He nodded and took the seat as she settled back into the tube. "What do you want me to do?"

"Very little, I hope. The procedure's pretty straightforward. You ready?" she asked, not turning her head to face him.

He gazed at the screen, willing but baffled by the multiple options and instructions. "I guess so. What do I do now?"

"Ignore the technospeak. There's an option menu at the bottom."

His eyes dropped and he found himself nodding. "I see it. What next?"

"Hit either *B* or *C*. What's *C*?"

He studied the glowing print. "Display biofunctions."

"That's it."

On his command the screen was replaced by another,

no less complicated than its predecessor. "Okay, now I've got a whole page of new turkeytalk."

"Same procedure. Menu at the bottom. There should be a *V* command, for visual display. Hit it."

He complied, glancing back toward the cylinder.

Within the claustrophobic confines of the tube a small motor began to hum. Ripley shifted uncomfortably on the cushioned pallet, feeling very much like a bug under a microscope. Her surroundings suddenly pressed close around her, the wall and ceiling of the EEV threatening to collapse and pin her forever in place. She concentrated on keeping her heartbeat regular, her breathing steady as she closed her eyes. It helped, a little.

The display monitor in front of Aaron flickered. The incomprehensible technical information vanished, to be replaced by an in-depth medical percep scan of the inside of Ripley's head.

"Okay," he told her, "we're hot. I'm looking at your brain. The scanner's also printing a lot of information next to the image, and there's all sorts of option switches at the bottom of the screen."

"They're to make the scan system-specific," she heard herself telling him. "You know—nervous system, circulatory. Like that. Let's keep it as general as possible. Leave everything alone."

"No problem there." He stared in fascination at the screen. "What am I supposed to be looking for? I don't know how to read this stuff."

"Ignore the printouts and concentrate on the visuals," she told him. "Where is it now?"

"Moving down your neck. Am I supposed to see something?"

"If it's there, you'll know it when you see it."

"Okay, but it all looks normal to me so far. Of course, I'm not Clemens."

"Don't worry about it," she told him. "You won't have to be."

She could hear the soft whine of the scanner as it moved down her body, sliding smoothly on its hidden track somewhere deep within the instrument-packed cryotube. Even though there was no actual physical contact between her and the instrument, she found herself twitching slightly at its perceived presence. Whoever said there was no link between imagination and physicality had never spent any time in cryogenic deep sleep.

"Upper chest now," Aaron was saying. "I can see the tops of you lungs. Heart coming into view."

Despite her determination she found herself tensing uncontrollably. The muscles of her right forearm began to twitch spasmodically. The acting superintendent's voice buzzed in her ears, a lethal drone.

"Full chest view, at least according to what it says here. Heart and lungs seem to be functioning normally. Moving down."

The twitching stopped, her breathing eased. "Are you sure?"

"Hey, I don't see anything. If you'd give me an idea what I'm supposed to be looking for . . . maybe I missed it."

"No." Her mind was working furiously. "No, you didn't miss it."

"How do we get some enhancement?"

"Try *B*."

He complied, to no avail. "Nothing." He tried again, muttering to himself. "I gotta get a better angle."

The instrumentation hummed. Suddenly he paused.

"Holy shit—" He broke off, eyes bulging as he leaned toward the screen.

"What?" she demanded. "What is it?"

"I don't know how to tell you this. I think you got one inside you."

He stared at the screen in disbelief. The embryonic creature was definitely kin to the monster that had destroyed the men . . . and yet it was also distinctively, subtly different.

It wasn't fair, she thought. She'd known, she'd more than suspected, for days. Then her chest scan had come through clean, giving her hope. Now this, the ultimate morbid revelation. Still, it wasn't a shock.

Now that her suspicions were confirmed she felt oddly liberated. The future was no longer in doubt. She could proceed, confident in the knowledge that she was taking the right course. The only course.

"What's it look like?"

"Fucking horrible," Aaron told her, at once repelled and fascinated by what he was seeing. "Like one of them, only small. Maybe a little different."

"Maybe? Are you sure?"

"I'm not sure of anything. I didn't hang around to take pictures of the big one."

"Keyboard," she told him. "Hit the pause button."

"Already did. The scanner's stopped moving."

"Now move the screen. I've got to take a look."

The acting superintendent hesitated, looking toward the cryotube and its recumbent occupant. "I don't think you want to."

"It's my choice. Do it."

His lips tightened. "Okay. If you think you're ready."

"I didn't say I was ready. Just do it."

He adjusted the viewscreen, waiting while she took a long, unblinking look.

"Okay. That's enough." Aaron instantly deactivated the scanner.

"I'm sorry," he murmured as gently as he could. "I don't know what to say. Anything I can do—"

"Yeah." She started struggling against the confines of the tube. "Help me get out of here." Her arms were extended upward, reaching toward him.

- XIII -

The assembly hall looked emptier than ever with its reduced population of prisoners. The men muttered and argued among themselves as Dillon's fist slammed into the transparent window on the wall. Reaching in, he ripped free the loosely secured fire axe within and turned to hold it over his head.

"Give us strength, O lord, to endure. Until the day. Amen."

Fists rose into the air. The men were uncertain, but determined. Dillon surveyed them intently.

"It's loose. It's out there. A rescue team is on the way with the guns and shit. Right now there isn't anyplace that's real safe. I say we stay here. No overhead vent shafts. If it comes in, it's gotta be through the door. We post a guard to let us know if it's comin'. In any case, lay low. Be ready and stay right, in case your time comes."

"Bullshit, man," said prisoner David. "We'll all be trapped in here like rats."

Dillon glared at him. "Most of you got blades stashed away. Get 'em out."

"Right." William grunted. "You think we're gonna stab that motherfucker to death?"

"I don't think shit," Dillon told him. "Maybe you can hurt it while you're checkin' out. It's something. You got any better ideas?"

William did not. Nor did anyone else.

"I'm tellin' you," Dillon continued, "until that rescue team gets here, we're in the shit. Get prepared."

"I ain't stayin' here." William was already backing away. "You can bet on it."

Dillon turned, spat to his left. "Suit yourself."

Aaron tapped out the necessary code, then ran his thumb over the identiprint. The inner door which protected central communications slid aside, telltales coming to life on the board, the screen clearing obediently as the system awaited input.

"Okay," he told the woman hovering nearby, "what do you want to send?"

"You got a line back to the Network?"

His brows furrowed as he checked the readouts. "Yeah, it's up. What do you want to say?"

"I want to tell them the whole place has gone toxic. I think they'll buy it. There's enough refining waste lying around to make it believable."

He gaped at her. "Are you kidding? Tell them that and they won't come here. Not until they can run and check out the results of a remote inspection, anyway. The rescue team'll turn back."

"Exactly."

"What are you talking about? We're like dead fish in a market waiting here. Our only hope is that they arrive in time to kill this fucker before it gets the rest of us. And maybe they can do something for you. You think of that? You're so sure this thing can beat anything they've got, but you don't know that for a fact. Maybe they can freeze you, do some kind of operation.

"You said that they've been accumulating information on it. You think they'd be coming to try and take one back if they didn't think they could contain it? Hell, we contained it and we weren't even ready for it. They'll be all set up to try a capture. They got the technology."

She remained adamant. "All the Company's got is greed for brains. I know. I've dealt with them and I've dealt with the aliens and frankly I'm not so sure that in the long run the Company isn't the greater threat. I can't take the chance. All I know for certain is that if one of these things gets off this planet it'll kill everything. That's what it's designed to do: kill and multiply.

"We can't let the Company come here. They'll do everything in their power to take it back with them." She made a disgusted noise. "For profit."

"Fuck you. I'm sorry as hell you got this thing inside you, lady, but I want to get rescued. I guess I've got more confidence in the Company than you. As it happens, I don't think you're looking at the situation rationally, and I suppose you've got plenty of reasons not to. But that doesn't mean I have to see things the same way, and I don't.

"I don't give a shit about these meatball prisoners. They can kill the thing or avoid it and howl holy hosannas to the heavens until they drop dead, but I got a wife and kid. Married real young so that despite the time distortions we'd still have quality time together when I finished my tour here. I was set to go back on the next rotation. Because of all this I can maybe claim extenuating hazards and go back with the rescue ship. I'll collect full-term pay and probably a bonus. If that happens you could say that your xenomorph's done me a favor.''

"I'm sorry. Look, I know this is hard for you,'' she told him, trying to keep a rein on her temper, "but I've got to send a message back. There's a hell of a lot more at stake here than your personal visions of happy suburban retirement. If the alien gets loose on Earth your sappy fantasies won't be worth crap.''

"I'll put my trust in the Company,'' he said firmly.

"Dammit, Aaron, I need the code!''

He leaned back in the seat. "Sorry, mum. It's classified. Can't expect me to violate the regs, can you?''

She knew she didn't have much time and she was starting to lose it. Here she was, dealing with the Company attitude again—that closed, restricted corporate world where ethics and morals were conveniently masked by regulations.

"Look, shithead, you can screw you precious regulations. It's got to be done. Give it to me!''

"No fuckin' way, lady. You don't get the code out of me without killing me first.''

She bent toward him, then forced herself to ease off. Once again she found herself tired beyond imagining. Why was she driving herself like this? She didn't owe anybody anything, least of all the representatives of the Company. If they took the alien on board their ship and it killed all of them, what was that to her?

"Nothing personal, you understand,'' he was saying even as he was watching her carefully, alert for any sudden moves. He didn't think she posed him any real danger, but in the short time that he'd seen her operate he'd learned enough to know that it would be dangerous to underestimate her. "I think you're okay."

"Thanks." Her tone was flat, dulled.

"So that's settled. We're working together again." He was inordinately pleased. "Got any ideas?"

She turned and he tensed momentarily, but she kept going past him to the service counter and drew herself a glass of water. Her thirst was constant and not due to tension and nerves. Her body was supplying fluids for more than one.

"The worker-warrior won't kill me," she told him as she halted nearby.

His eyebrows rose. "Oh, yeah? Why not?"

She sipped at the glass. "It can't nail me without risking the health of the embryonic queen. And while I know that one of them can reproduce others of its kind, it may not be able to produce more than a single queen. Not enough of the right genetic material or something. I don't know that for a fact, but the proof is that it hasn't tried to kill me so far."

"You really want to bet this thing's that smart?"

"Smarts may not have anything to do with it. It may be pure instinct. Damage the host and you risk premature damage to the unborn queen. It makes sense." She met his gaze. "It could've killed me twice already, but it didn't. It knows what I'm carrying." She rubbed her chin thoughtfully.

"I'm going to find it," she announced suddenly. "We'll see how smart it is."

He gaped at her. "You're gonna go look for it?"

"Yeah. I got a pretty good idea where it is. It's just up there in the attic."

He frowned. "What attic? We don't have an attic."

"It's a metaphor." She finished the water.

"Oh." He was staring at her.

"Wanna come?"

He shook his head. She smiled, put the glass back in its holder, and turned to exit the communications room. Aaron followed her with his eyes.

"Fuck me," he murmured to no one in particular.

· XIV ·

The access corridor was empty. Pausing, she jammed the torch she'd been carrying into a seam in the wall, studying the line of aged, rusting pipes nearby. Grabbing the nearest, she braced herself and yanked hard. The metal snapped and bent toward her. A second yank broke it free. Satisfied, she continued on.

The infirmary seemed more deserted than ever. She paused for a look around, half expecting to see Clemens bent over his workstation, glancing up to grin in her direction. The computer was dark and silent, the chair empty.

It was hard to pull herself up into the overhead air duct while manipulating both the five-foot length of pipe and the flashlight, but she managed. The duct was dark and empty. Adjusting the battered flashlight for wide beam, she flashed it behind her before starting off in the opposite direction.

Exactly how long or how far she crawled before she started calling, she didn't know; only that the faint light from the infirmary had long since faded behind her. Her shouts were muted at first, then louder as fear gave way to anger. Her fate was inevitable. She just had to know. She had to see that thing face-to-face.

"Come on! I know you're here!" She advanced on hands and knees. "Come on. Just do what you do."

The air vent bent sharply to the left. She kept moving, alternately muttering and shouting. "Come on, you shithead. Where are you when I need you?"

Her knees were getting raw when she finally paused, listening intently. A noise? Or her own imagination, working overtime?

"Shit." She resumed her awkward, uncomfortable advance, turning another corner.

It opened into an alcove large enough to allow her to stand. Gratefully she climbed to her feet, stretching. The alcove was home to a decrepit, rusting water purification unit consisting of a thousand-gallon tank and a maze of neglected pipes.

Behind the tank the ventilation duct stretched off before her, an endless, difficult-to-negotiate tube of darkness. As she stared a fresh wave of nausea overcame her and she leaned against the tank for support.

As she did so an alien tail flicked out and knocked the flashlight from her fingers.

It landed on the concrete floor, spinning but staying lit. Ripley whirled, a feeling of desperation creeping up her spine.

The alien peered out at her from within the network of pipes and conduits where it had been resting. It regarded her.

"You fucker," she muttered as she gathered her strength. Then she rammed the metal pipe directly into its thorax.

With an echoing roar it exploded from behind the maze, metal pipes giving way like straws. Fully aroused and alert, it crouched directly in front of her, thick gelatinous saliva dripping from its outer jaws.

She held her ground, straightening. "Come on, fucker. Kill me!" When it didn't react she slammed at it again with the pipe.

With a roar it reached out and slapped the pipe away, stood glaring at her. Sweat pouring down her face, she continued to stare back.

Then it whirled and bolted into the darkness. She slumped, gazing after it.

"Bastard."

Dillon found the lieutenant in the assembly hall, seated by herself in the huge, deeply shadowed room. She sat with her head in her hands, utterly exhausted, utterly alone. The fire axe dangling from his right hand, he walked over and halted nearby. She must have been aware of his presence, but she did nothing to acknowledge it.

Ordinarily he would have respected her silence and moved on, but conditions had passed beyond ordinary.

"You okay?" She didn't reply, didn't look up.

"What are you doin' out here? You're supposed to be lyin' low like everybody else. What happens if that thing shows up?"

Her head rose. "It's not going to kill me."

"Why not?"

"Because I've got one of them inside of me. The big one won't kill its own."

Dillon stared at her. "Bullshit."

"Look, I saw it an hour ago. I stood right next to it. I

could've been lunch, but it wouldn't touch me. It ran away. It won't kill its future.''

"How do you know this thing's inside you?''

"I saw it on the cat-scan. It's a queen. It can make thousands like the one that's running around out there.''

"You mean like a queen bee?''

"Or ant. But, it's just an analogy. These creatures aren't insects. They just have a crudely analogous social structure. We don't know a great deal about them. As you may have noticed, they don't make for an easy study.''

"How do you know it's a queen?'' he found himself asking.

"For one thing, the shape of the skull is very distinct. It's backed by a large, upsweeping frill. The beginnings of that were clearly visible in the scanner images. For another, the gestation period for the warrior-worker analogs is quite short, in some cases only a day or so. They mature through their different stages with incredible speed.'' She looked rueful. "Very effective survival trait.

"If this was an ordinary worker it would have come out by now, emerging through the sternum region. Also, it's gestating in the uterine cavity instead of the chest. Since a queen is a much more complex organism it apparently requires both more space and time to mature. Otherwise I'd be dead by now.

"I've seen how they work. It's not very pretty. When full grown this thing is enormous, much bigger than the one we've been fighting here. It's definitely going to be a queen, an egg layer. Millions of eggs. It's not going to be anything like the one that's out there running around loose.'' Her voice fell. "Like I said, nobody's had any experience with a larval queen. I don't know how long a gestation period it requires, except that it's self-evidently a lot longer than an ordinary_worker.''

He gazed down at her. "Still sounds like bullshit to me. If you got this thing inside you, how'd it get there?''

She was staring down at her hands. "While I was in deep sleep. I guess the horrible dream I had wasn't exactly a dream. I got raped, though I don't know that that's a wholly accurate term. Rape is an act of premeditated violence. This was an act of procreation, even if my participation wasn't voluntary. We would call it rape, but I doubt that the creature would. It would probably find the concept . . . well, alien.'' She looked thoughtful, thinking back.

"The one that got loose on my first ship, the *Nostromo*, was making preparations to reproduce itself, but it wasn't a queen either. At least some of them must be hermaphroditic. Self-fertilizing, so that even one isolated individual can perpetuate the species. A warrior-worker is capable of producing eggs, but only slowly, one at a time, until it can develop a queen to take over the job. That's how this one was able to start a queen inside me. At least, that's the best scenario I can come up with. I'm no xenologist.''

She hesitated. "Great, huh? I get to be the mother of the mother of the apocalypse. I can't do what I should. So you've got to help. You've got to kill me.''

He took a step backward. "What the fuck you talkin' about?''

"You don't get it, do you? I'm finished. I'm dead the minute it's born because I'll no longer be necessary to its continued survival. I've seen it happen. That I can live with, if it's not too strict a contradiction in terms. I've been ready to die ever since I encountered the first one of these things. But I will be damned if I'm going to let those idiots from Weyland-Yutani take it back to Earth. They just might succeed, and that would be it for the rest of mankind. Maybe for all life on the planet. I don't see why these things wouldn't be able to reproduce in any animal of a size larger than, say, a cat.

"It has to die, and in order for that to happen somebody's got to kill me. You up to it?"

"You don't have to worry about that."

"It's kind of funny, in a way. I've done so much killing lately and now I find I can't manage just one more. Maybe because I've had to concentrate so hard on surviving. So you've got to help me." She met his gaze unwaveringly.

"Just do it. No speeches." She turned her back on him. "Come on," she urged him, "do it! You're supposed to be a killer . . . kill me. Come on, Dillon. Push yourself. Look back. I think you can do it, you big, ugly son of a bitch."

He studied her slim form, the pale neck and slumped shoulders. A single well-directed blow would do it, cut through her spinal cord and vertebrae quick and clean. Death would be almost instantaneous. Then he could turn his attention to her belly, to the monstrous organism growing inside. Drag the corpse to the smelter and dump it all in the furnace. It would all be over and done with in a couple of minutes. He raised the axe.

The muscles in his face and arms tightened convulsively and the axe made a faint whooshing sound as it cut through the stale air. He brought it down and around full force . . . to slam into the wall next to her head. She jerked at the impact, then blinked and whirled on him.

"What the hell is this? You're not doing me any favors."

"I don't like losin' a fight, not to nobody, not to nothin'. The big one out there's already killed half my guys, got the other half scared shitless. As long as it's alive, you're not saving any universe."

"What's wrong? I thought you were a killer."

"I want to get this thing and I need you to do it. If it won't kill you, then maybe that helps us fight it." She stared at him helplessly. "Otherwise, fuck you. Go kill yourself."

"We knock its ass off, then you'll kill me?"

"No problem. Quick, painless, easy." He reached up to tear the axe out of the wall.

The remaining men had assembled in the main hall. Aaron stood off to one side, sipping something from a tumbler. Dillon and Ripley stood side by side in the center, confronting the others.

"This is the choice," the big man was telling them. "You die sitting here on your ass, or maybe you die out there. But at least we take a shot at killing it. We owe it one. It's fucked us over. Maybe we get even for the others. Now, how do you want it?"

Morse eyed him in disbelief. "What the fuck are you talkin' about?"

"Killin' that big motherfucker."

Aaron took a step forward, suddenly uneasy. "Hold it. There's a rescue team on the way. Why don't we just sit it out?"

Ripley eyed him narrowly. "Rescue team for who?"

"For us."

"Bullshit," she snapped. "All they want's the beast. You know that."

"I don't give a damn what they want. They aren't gonna kill us."

"I'm not so sure. You don't know the Company the way I do."

"Come on. They're gonna get us out of here, take us home."

"They ain't gonna take *us* home," Dillon observed.

"That still doesn't mean we should go out and fight it," Morse whined. "Jesus Christ, give me a break."

Aaron shook his head slowly. "You guys got to be fucking nuts. I got a wife. I got a kid. I'm going home."

Dillon's expression was hard, unyielding, and his tone smacked of unpleasant reality. "Get real. Nobody gives a shit about you, Eight-five. You are not one of us. You are not a believer. You are just a Company man."

"That's right," Aaron told him. "I'm a Company man and not some fucking criminal. You keep telling me how dumb I am, but I'm smart enough not to have a life sentence on this rock, and I'm smart enough to wait for some firepower to show up before we get out and fight this thing."

"Right. Okay. You just sit here on your ass. It's fine."

Morse's head jerked. "How about if I sit here on my ass?"

"No problem," Dillon assured him. "I forgot. You're the guy that's got a deal with God to live forever. And the rest of you pussies can sit out too. Me and her"—he indicated Ripley—"we'll do all the fighting."

Morse hesitated, found some of the others gazing at him. He licked his lower lip. "Okay. I'm with you. I want it to die. I hate the fucker. It killed my friends, too. But why can't we wait a few hours and have the fuckin' company techs with guns on our side? Why the shit do we have to make some fucking suicide run?"

"Because they won't kill it," Ripley informed him.

"They may kill you just for having seen it, but they won't kill *it*."

"That's crazy." Aaron was shaking his head again. "Just horseshit. They won't kill us."

"Think not?" She grinned wolfishly. "The first time they heard about this thing it was crew expendable. The second time they sent some marines: they were expendable. What makes you think they're gonna care about a bunch of double-Y chromos at the back end of space? Do you really think they're gonna let you interfere with advanced Company weapons research? They think you're crud, all of you. They don't give a damn about one friend of yours that died. Not one." There was silence when she'd finished. Then someone in the back spoke up.

"You got some kind of plan?"

Dillon studied his companions, his colleagues in hell. "This is a refinery as well as a mine, isn't it? The thing's afraid of fire, ain't it? All we have to do is get the fuckin' beast into the big mold, pour hot metal on it."

He kicked a stool across the floor. "You're all gonna die. Only question is when. This is as good a place to take your first step to heaven as any. It's ours. It ain't much, but it's ours. Only question in life is how you check out. Now, you want it on your feet, or on your knees beggin'? I ain't much for beggin'. Nobody never gave me nothin'. So I say, fuck it. Let's fight."

The men looked at one another, each waiting for someone else to break the silence that ensued. When it finally happened, the responses came fast and confident.

"Yeah, okay. I'm in."

"Why not? We ain't got nothin' to lose."

"Yeah . . . okay . . . right . . . I'm in."

A voice rose higher. "Let's kick its fuckin' ass."

Someone else smiled. "You hold it, I'll kick it."

"Fuck it," snapped Morse finally. "Let's go for it."

Somehow they got some of the lights on in the corridors. It wasn't a question of power; the central fusion plant provided plenty of that. But there were terminals and switches and controls that hadn't been maintained for years in the damp climate of Fiorina. So some corridors and access ways had light while others continued to dwell in darkness.

Ripley surveyed the molding chamber thoughtfully as Dillon and prisoner Troy crowded close. Troy was the most technically oriented of the survivors, having enjoyed a brief career as a successful engineer before having the misfortune to find his wife and superior in the sack together. He'd murdered both of them, with all the technical skill he'd been able to muster. Faint howls of temporary insanity had bought him a ticket to Fiorina.

Now he demonstrated how the controls worked, which instruments were critical to the chamber's operation. Ripley watched and listened, uncertain.

"When was the last time you used this thing?"

"We fired it up five, six years ago. Routine maintenance check. That was the last time."

She pursed her lips. "Are you sure the piston's working?"

It was Dillon who replied. "Nothin's for sure. Includin' you."

"All I can say is that the indicators are all positive." Troy shrugged helplessly. "It's the best we've got."

"Remember," Dillon reminded them both, "we trap it here first. We hit the release, start the piston, then the piston will shove the motherfucker right into the mold. This is a high-tech cold-stamp facility. End of his ass. End of story."

Ripley eyed him. "What if someone screws up?"

"Then we're fucked," Dillon informed her calmly. "We've got one chance. One shot at this, that's all. You'll never have time to reset. Remember, when you hit the release, for a few seconds you're gonna be trapped in here with that fucking thing."

She nodded. "I'll do it. You guys don't drop the ball, I won't."

Dillon studied her closely. "Sister, you'd better be right about that thing not wanting you. Because if it wants out, that's how it's gonna go. Right through you."

She just stared back. "Save you some work, wouldn't it?" Troy blinked at her, but there was no time for questions.

"Where you gonna be?" she asked the big man.

"I'll be around."

"What about the others? Where are they?"

"Praying."

The survivors spread out, working their way through the corridors, head-butting the walls to pump themselves up, cursing and whooping. They no longer cared if the monster heard them. Indeed, they wanted it to hear them.

Torchlight gleamed off access ways and tunnels, throwing nervous but excited faces into sharp relief. Prisoner Gregor peered out of an alcove to see his buddy William deep in prayer.

"Hey Willie? You believe in this heaven shit?"

The other man looked up. "I dunno."

"Me neither."

"Fuck it. What else we gonna believe in? Bit late, now we're stuck here."

"Yeah, ain't that the truth? Well, hey, what the fuck, right?" He laughed heartily and they both listened to the echoes as they boomed back and forth down the corridor, amplified and distorted.

Morse heard them all: distant reverberations of nervous laughter, of terror and near hysteria. He pressed the switch that would activate the door he'd been assigned to monitor. It whined . . . and jammed partway open. Swallowing nervously, he leaned through the gap.

"Hey, guys? Hold it, hold it. I don't know about this shit. Maybe we should rethink this. I mean, my fuckin' door ain't workin' right. Guys?"

There was no response from down the corridor.

Farther up, Gregor turned to face his companion. "What the fuck's he saying?"

"Shit, I dunno," said William with a shrug.

Prisoner Kevin held the long-burning flare out in front of him as he felt his way along the corridor wall. There was another man behind him, and behind him another, and so on for a substantial length of the tunnel. None were in sight now, though, and his nerves were jumping like bowstrings.

"Hey, you hear something?" he murmured to anyone who might happen to be within earshot. "I heard Morse. Sounded kinda—"

The scream silenced him. It was so near it was painful. His legs kept moving him forward, as though momentary mental paralysis had yet to reach the lower half of his body.

Ahead, the alien was dismembering a friend of his named Vincent, who no longer had anything to scream with. He hesitated only briefly.

"Come and get me, you fucker!"

Obligingly, the monster dropped the piece of Vincent it was holding and charged.

Kevin had been something of an athlete in his day. Those memories returned with a rush as he tore back up the corridor. Couple years back there wasn't a man he'd met he couldn't outrun. But he wasn't racing a man now. The inhuman apparition was closing fast, even as he accelerated to a sprint. The slower he became, the faster his hellacious pursuer closed.

He all but threw himself at the switch, whirling as he did so, his back slamming into the corridor wall, his chest heaving like a bellows. The steel door it controlled slammed shut.

Something crashed into it a bare second after it sealed, making a huge dent in the middle. He slumped slightly and somehow found the wind to gasp aloud, "Door C9 . . . closed!"

At the other end of the recently traversed passageway prisoner Jude appeared, no mop in hand now. Instead he held his own flare aloft, illuminating the corridor.

"Yoo-hoo. Hey, fuckface, come and get me. Take your best shot."

Confounded by the unyielding door, the alien pivoted at the sound and rushed in its direction. Jude took off running, not as fast as Kevin but with a bigger head start. The alien closed fast. Once again, seconds were the difference. The closing doorway separated it from its prey.

On the other side of the barrier Jude struggled to regain his wind. "Over in the east wing: door B7. Safe."

An instant later an alien foreleg smashed through the small glass window set in the steel. Screaming, Jude scrabbled backward along the wall, away from the clutching, frantic claws.

Dillon stood alone in the corridor he'd chosen to patrol and muttered to himself, "It's started."

"It's in tunnel B," Morse was yelling as he ran down his own private passageway. "Must be heading over to channel A!"

At an intersection, William nearly ran over Gregor as

the two men joined up. "I heard it," Gregor muttered. "Channel E, dammit."

"Did you say B?"

"No, E."

William frowned as he ran. "We're supposed to stay—"

"Move your fucking ass!" In no mood to debate what their theoretical relative positions ought to have been, Gregor accelerated wordlessly. William trailed in his wake.

In a side corridor Jude linked up with Kevin, and they glanced knowingly at the other. "You too?"

"Yeah." Kevin was fighting for air.

"Okay. Over to E. Everybody."

Kevin made a face, trying to remember. "Where the fuck's E?"

His companion gestured impatiently. "This way. Get a fuckin' move-on."

David was still alone, and he didn't relish the continuing solitude. According to plan, he should have linked up with someone else by now. He did, however, find what remained of Vincent. It slowed but did not halt him.

"Kevin? Gregor? Morse? I found Vincent." There was no response. He kept moving, unwilling to stop for anyone or anything. "Let's shut this fucker down." The section of tunnel directly ahead was darker than the one he'd just vacated, but at least it was empty.

In the main corridor Dillon glanced at Troy. "Help them."

The other prisoner nodded and headed into the maze of corridors, hefting his map.

Prisoner Eric stood nearby, his gaze shifting constantly from Dillon to Ripley. He chewed his lower lip, then his fingernails.

*   *   *

She studied the monitor panel. It showed Gregor going one way, Morse the other. Her expression twisted.

"Where the fuck is he going? Why don't they stick to the plan?"

"You're immune," Dillon reminded her. "They're not."

"Well, what the hell are they doin'?"

Dillon's attention was focused on the dimly lit far end of the corridor. "Improvising."

She rested her hand on the main piston control, saw Eric staring at her. He was sweating profusely.

David stumbled through the darkened corridor, holding his flare aloft and trying to penetrate the blackness ahead.

"Here, kitty, kitty, kitty. Here—" He broke off. The alien was clearly visible at the far end, pounding ineffectually on the door through which Jude had recently vanished.

He cocked his arm as the alien turned. "Here, pussycat. Playtime!" He heaved the hissing flare. The alien was already coming toward him before the flare struck the floor.

Turning, he raced at high speed back the way he'd come. The distance to the next barrier was relatively short and he felt confident he'd make it. Sure enough, he was through in plenty of time. His hand came down hard on the close button. The door slipped downward . . . and stopped.

His eyes widened and he made a soft mewling noise as he stumbled backward, one faltering step at a time.

As he stared, the door continued to descend in halting jerks. He quivered as the alien slammed full speed into the door. Metal buckled but continued to descend in its uneven, herky-jerky fashion.

An alien paw punched through the gap and made a grab at David's leg. Screaming, he leapt onto a ledge in the corridor wall. The hand continued to flail around, hunting for him, as the door jerked down, down. At the last instant the foreleg withdrew.

There was silence in the corridor.

It took him a long moment to find his voice and when he did, what emerged was little more than a terrified whimper.

"Door 3, channel F. Shut . . . I hope."

Morse didn't hear him as he continued to stumble blindly down his own corridor. "Kevin? Gregor? Where the fuck are you? Where is everybody? K, L, M, all locked and secured." He glanced at a plate set into the wall. "I'm back in A."

In a side passageway Gregor was likewise counting panels. "Channel V secure. Channel P holding."

Behind him William struggled to keep pace. "Did you say P or D?" he shouted. "For fuck's sake—"

Gregor turned without stopping. "Shut the fuck up! Move!"

Unsure of his position, Kevin discovered that he'd doubled back on himself. "Shit. I'm in R. That's safe. That's safe. Isn't it?"

Jude overheard, raised his voice so his companion could hear. "You forgot, man. R leads back into F. I'm moving through F right now. Gonna shut it down."

Disoriented, Troy halted at an intersection. He'd moved too fast, ignoring the map and trusting to memory. Now he found himself appraising the multiple tunnels uncertainly.

"Channel F? Where the fuck— There ain't no fuckin' Channel F."

He moved forward, hesitated, and chose the corridor to his immediate right, instead.

That corridor, however, was already occupied by another frustrated inhabitant.

Dillon and Ripley heard the distant screams. As usual, the screams didn't last for very long.

"Morse?" Dillon called out. "Kevin, Gregor?"

Ripley strained to see past him. "What's going on back there?"

The big man glanced tensely back at her. "All they have to do is run down the damn corridors." He hefted his axe and started forward. "Stay here."

The side corridor from which they expected their visitor remained deserted. No alien. No people. Only distant, echoing voices, some distinctly panicky.

Behind him, Eric voiced his thoughts aloud. "Where in hell is it?" Dillon just glanced at him.

Sucking up his courage, David moved back to the door and peered through the small window. The corridor beyond was empty. He raised his voice.

"I've lost him. Don't know where the fucking thing is. Not gonna open the door. I think it went up in the fucking air vent." He turned slowly to inspect the single air vent in the tunnel above him.

He was right.

Ripley waited until the last of the echoes faded to silence. Eric had been moving forward, his eyes harbingers of imminent collapse. If someone didn't do something he was going to break and take off running. There was nowhere to run to. She moved toward him, caught his gaze, trying to stare him down, to transfer some of her own confidence into him.

Dillon had disappeared down the side corridor. It didn't take him long to find Troy's remains. After a quick look around he retreated back the way he'd come.

Morse and Jude had finally linked up. They ran along side by side . . . until Jude slipped and went down hard. His fingers fumbled at the warm, sticky mess which had tripped him up.

"For fuck's sake . . . yuck."

When Jude lifted it toward the flare for a better look, Morse recoiled in horror. Then he got a good look at what he'd picked up, and they screamed in unison.

Ripley listened intently, momentarily forgetting Eric. The screams were close now—immediate, not echoes. Suddenly the prisoner whirled and rushed back toward the piston control. She ran after him . . .

As the alien appeared, racing across the corridor.

Eric's fingers started to convulse on the control and she barely had time to grab his hand.

"Wait! It's not in position yet!" With an effort of will she managed to block him from releasing the piston.

That was all it took. Defeated mentally as well as physically, he slumped back, exhausted and trembling.

Kevin moved slowly through the corridor. He was getting close to the piston alcove now, as safe a place as any. He'd done everything that had been asked of him. They couldn't ask for more, not now.

Something made him look up. The alien positioned in the vent above didn't bother to drop. Instead it reached down and snatched him up as easily as if it had been fishing for a frog. Blood splattered.

At the far end of the passageway Dillon appeared. Spotting Kevin's jerking legs he rushed forward and threw both arms around the twitching knees. It was something the alien wasn't prepared for and the two men dropped.

Ripley saw Dillon drag the wounded prisoner into the

main corridor. With a glance at the useless Eric she started
forward to help.

Blood spurted from the injured man's neck. Whipping
off her jacket, she wrapped it around the wound as tightly as
she could. The blood slowed, but not enough. Dillon held
the man close, murmuring.

"No death, only—"

There was no time to finish the prayer. The alien
emerged from the side access. Ripley rose and started
backing away.

"Leave the body. Draw it in."

Dillon nodded and joined her, the two of them retreating
toward the control alcove.

The alien watched. They were moving slowly, with
nowhere to retreat to. There was still life in the damaged
figure on the floor. The alien jumped forward to finish the
job.

Spinning, Ripley made a slashing gesture in Eric's
direction. Eric erupted from his hiding place and slammed
his hand down on the control.

The piston shot forward, sweeping up both Kevin's
body and that of the alien, shunting them toward the gap
which led to the furnace. Heat and howling air filled the
corridor.

But the alien had vanished.

Sweating, Ripley took a step forward. "Where the
hell's it gone?"

"Shit!" Dillon tried to peer around the machinery. "It
must be behind the fucking piston."

"Behind it?" She gaped at him.

"Seal the doors," he bellowed. "We gotta get it
back!" They exchanged a glance, then took off in opposite
directions.

"Jude, Morse!" Dillon pounded down the corridor he'd chosen, searching for survivors. Meanwhile Ripley went in search of Eric and William. Found them, too, all mixed up together and no longer worrying. About anything. She continued on.

Morse was creeping now, no longer running. Hearing a noise, he paused to check the side access way from which it had come, exhaled at the sight of nothing. He began retracing his steps, keeping his eyes forward.

Until he bumped into something soft and animate.

"What the—!"

It was Jude. Equally startled, the other man whirled, displaying the scissors he carried like a weapon. Simultaneously relieved and furious, Morse grabbed the twin blades and angled them upward.

"Not like this. Like this, moron." He whacked the other man on the side of the head. Jude blinked, nodded, and started off in the other direction.

Dillon was back in the main corridor, yelling. "Jude, Jude!" The other man heard him, hesitated.

The alien was right behind him.

He ran like hell, toward Dillon, who urged him on.

"Don't look back. As fast you fucking can!"

Jude came on, trying, trying for his life. But he wasn't Kevin, or Gregor. The alien caught him. Blood exploded against the door that Dillon desperately sent slamming shut.

In the next corridor Ripley heard, growled to herself. Time was ticking away as the piston continued its inexorable and currently useless slide forward.

Gregor screamed for help, but there was no one around to hear him. He raced blindly down the passageway, ricocheting off the corners like a pinball until he slammed into Morse, running hard the other way. Nervous, then half laughing, they picked themselves up, staring in relief at one another.

Until the alien flashed past and smashed into Gregor in midlaugh, tearing him apart.

Blood and pulp showering his face and torso, Morse fought to scramble away, screaming for mercy to something that neither understood nor cared about his desperation. He could only stare as the creature methodically eviscerated Gregor's corpse. Then he crawled frantically.

He bumped into something unyielding and his head whipped around. Feet. His head tilted back. Ripley's feet.

She threw the flare she was holding at the alien as it tried to duck into an air vent. The burning magnesium alloy forced it to drop Gregor's ravaged body.

"Come on, you bastard!"

As Morse looked on in fascination, the alien, instead of rushing forward to decapitate the lieutenant, coiled up against the far wall. She advanced, ignoring its cringing and spitting.

"Come on. I got what you want. Follow me. I want to show you something. Come on, damn you!"

The alien's tail flicked out and lashed at her. Not hard enough to kill; just enough to fend her off.

At that moment Dillon arrived in the doorway, staring. She whirled on him. "Get back! Don't get in the way!"

The alien resumed its attack posture, turning to face the newcomer. Desperately Ripley inserted herself between it and Dillon, who suddenly realized not only what was happening but what she was trying to do.

Moving up behind, he grabbed her and held her tight.

The alien went berserk, but kept its distance as the two humans retreated, Ripley tight in Dillon's grasp.

It followed them into the main corridor, keeping the

distance between them constant, waiting. Dillon glanced toward the waiting mold, called out.

"In here, stupid!"

The alien hesitated, then leapt to the ceiling and scuttled over the doorjamb.

"Shut it!" Ripley said frantically. "Now!"

Dillon didn't need to be told. He activated the door in front of her. It slammed tight, imprisoned them both in the main corridor with the creature.

Morse appeared behind it, saw what was happening. "Get out! Get the fuck out now!"

Ripley yelled back at him. "Close the door!" The other man hesitated. As he did so, the alien turned toward him. "Now!"

Morse jerked forward and hit the switch. The door rammed down, sealing them off from his position. A moment later the piston appeared, continuing on its cleansing passage and obscuring them from view.

He turned and ran back the way he'd come.

Within the main corridor the piston crunched into the alien, knocking it backward. Forgetting now about the two humans, it turned and sought to squeeze a leg past the heavy barrier. There was no room, no space at all. The piston continued to force it toward the mold.

Dillon and Ripley were already there. End of the line. Nowhere else to go.

Morse scrambled up the ladder which lead to the crane cab, wondering if he remembered enough to activate it. He'd have to. There was no time to consult manuals, and no one left to ask.

The massive landing craft disdained the use of the mine's ill-maintained landing port. Instead it set down on the gravel outside, the backwash of its maneuvering engines sending dirt and rocks flying. Moments later heavily armed men and women were rushing toward the facility's main entrance.

From within the lock Aaron watched them disembark, a broad smile on his face. They had smart guns and armor piercers, thermoseeking rails and rapid-fire handguns. They knew what they'd be up against and they'd come prepared. He straightened his uniform as best as he could and prepared to pop the lock.

"I knew they'd make it." He raised his voice. "Hey, over here! This way!" He started to activate the lock mechanism.

He never got the chance. The door exploded inward, six commandos and two medical officers rushing through even before the dust had settled. All business, the commandos spread out to cover the lock area. Aaron moved forward, thinking as he did so the captain in their midst was a dead ringer for the dead android that had been on the lieutenant's lifeboat.

"Right, sir," he announced as he stopped in front of the officer and snapped off a crisp salute. "Warder Aaron, 137512."

The captain ignored him. "Where is Lieutenant Ripley? Is she still alive?"

A little miffed at the indifference but still eager to be of help, Aaron replied quickly. "Right, sir. If she's alive, she's in the mold. They're all in the leadworks with the beast, sir. Absolute madness. Wouldn't wait. I tried to tell 'em—"

The officer cut him off abruptly. "You've seen this beast?"

"Right, sir. Horrible. Unbelievable. She's got one inside her."

"We know that." He nodded tersely in the direction of the commandos. "We'll take over now. Show us where you last saw her."

Aaron nodded, eagerly led them into the depths of the complex.

Ripley and Dillon continued retreating into the mold until there was ceramic alloy at their backs and nowhere else to stand. A grinding of gears caught her attention and her head jerked back. Overhead she could see machinery moving as the refinery responded inexorably to its programmed sequence.

"Climb," she told her companion. "It's our only chance!"

"What about you?" Dillon spoke as the alien entered the back part of the mold, forced along by the massive piston.

"It won't kill me."

"Bullshit! There's gonna be ten tons of hot metal in here!"

"Good! I keep telling you I want to die."

"Yeah, but I don't—"

Soon the alien would be on top of them. "Now's your chance," Ripley shouted. "Get going!"

He hesitated, then grabbed her. "I'm taking you with me!" He shoved her bodily upward.

Despite her resistance he managed to climb. Seeing that he wasn't going to go without her she reluctantly started to follow suit, moving in front of him up the side of the mold. The alien turned away from the piston, spotted them, and followed.

At the top of the mold Ripley secured herself on the edge and reached down to help Dillon. The pursuing alien's inner jaws shot out, reaching. Dillon kicked down, slashing with the fire axe.

Ripley continued her ascent as Dillon fought off the pursuit. More noise drew her attention to the now functioning gantry crane. She could see Morse inside, cursing and hammering at the controls.

The Company squad appeared on the crest of the observation platform, their leader taking in all of what was happening below at a glance. Morse saw them shouting at him, ignored them as he frantically worked controls.

The container of now molten alloy bubbled as it was tipped.

"Don't do it!" the captain of the new arrivals shouted. 'No!''

The alien was very close now, but not quite close enough. Not quite. White-hot liquid metal poured past Ripley and Dillon, a torrent of intense heat that forced both of them to cover their faces with their hands. The metallic cascade struck the alien and knocked it screeching back into the mold, sweeping it away as flames leaped in all directions.

High above, Morse stood and stared down through the window of the crane, his expression a mask of satisfaction.

"Eat shit, you miserable fucker!"

Dillon joined Ripley on the edge of the mold, both of them staring downward as they shielded their faces against the heat rising from the pool of bubbling metal. Suddenly her attention was drawn by movement across the way.

"They're here!" She clutched desperately at her companion. "Keep your promise!"

Dillon stared at her. "You mean it."

"Yes! I've got it inside me! Quit fucking around!"

Uncertainly, he put his hands around her throat.

She stared at him angrily. "Do it!"

His fingers tightened. A little pressure, a twist, and her neck would snap. That was all it would take. A moment of effort, of exertion. It wasn't as if he didn't know how, as if he hadn't done it before, a long time ago.

"I can't!" The denial emerged from his throat half cry, half croak. "I can't do it!" He looked at her almost pleadingly.

His expression turned to one of horror as he turned around, only to confront the burning and smoking alien. Resigned, he allowed himself to be pulled into its embrace, the two of them vanishing beneath the roiling surface of the molten metal. Ripley looked on in astonishment, at once repelled and fascinated. An instant later the curving alien skull reappeared. Dripping molten metal, it began to haul itself out of the mold.

Looking around wildly, she spotted the emergency chain. It was old and corroded, as might be the controls it activated. Not that it mattered. There was nothing else. She wrenched on it.

Water erupted from the large bore quencher that hung over the lip of the mold. She found herself tangled up in the chain, unable to get loose. The torrent of water drenched her, sweeping her around in tight spirals. But the chain would not let her go.

The cold water struck the alien and its hot metal coat. The head exploded first, then the rest of the body. Then the mold, vomiting chunks of supercooled metal and steam. Morse was thrown to the floor of the crane's cab as it rocked on its supports, while the commando unit ducked reflexively for cover.

Warm water and rapidly cooling metal rained down on the chamber.

When the deluge ended, the commando team resumed

its approach. But not before Ripley had swung herself up onto the crane platform, Morse reaching out to help her.

Once aboard, she leaned against the guard rail and gazed down into the furnace. Time again to be sick. The attacks of nausea and pain were coming more rapidly now.

She spotted the Company men coming up the stairs from below, heading for the crane. Aaron was in the forefront. She tried to escape but had no place to go.

"Don't come any closer," she shouted. "Stay where you are."

Aaron halted. "Wait. They're here to help."

She stared at him, pitying the poor simpleton. He had no idea what the stakes were, or what was likely to happen to him when the Company finally obtained what it was after. Except that that was not going to happen.

Another wave of nausea swept over her and she staggered against the railing. As she straightened, a figure stepped out from behind the heavily armed commandos. She gaped, uncertain at first of what she was seeing. It was a face she knew.

"Bishop?" she heard herself mumbling uncertainly.

He stopped, the others crowding close behind him, waiting for orders. The figure indicated they should relax. Then he turned to her, smiling reassuringly.

"I just want to help you. We're all on the same side."

"No more bullshit!" she snapped. Weak as she was, it took an effort to make the exclamation sound convincing. "I just felt the damn thing move."

As everyone present watched, she stepped farther out on the gantry platform. Something smacked into her lungs and she winced, never taking her eyes off the figure before her.

It was Bishop. No, not Bishop, but a perfect duplicate

of him. A completely in control, perfect down to the pores on his chin double of the sadly dismembered and cybernetically deceased Bishop. *Bishop II*, she told herself numbly. *Bishop Redux. Bishop to pawn four; Bishop takes Queen.*

Not as long as this lady's alive, she thought determinedly.

"You know who I am," the figure said.

"Yeah. A droid. Same model as Bishop. Sent by the fucking Company."

"I'm not the Bishop android. I designed it. I'm the prototype, so naturally I modeled its features after my own. I'm very human. I was sent here to show you a friendly face, and to demonstrate how important you are to us. To me. I've been involved with this project from the beginning. You mean a lot to me, Lieutenant Ripley. To a great many people. Please come down.

"I just want to help you. We have everything here to help you, Ripley." He gazed anxiously up at her. Now she recognized the outfits two of Bishop II's companions wore: they were biomedical technicians. It made her think of Clemens.

"Fuck you. I know all about 'friendly' Company faces. The last one I saw belonged to an asshole named Burke."

The man's smile faded. "Mr. Burke proved to be a poor choice to accompany your previous mission, an individual rather more interested in his own personal aggrandizement than in good Company policy. I assure you it was a mistake that will not be repeated. That is why I am here now instead of some inexperienced, overly ambitious underling."

"And you, of course, have no personal ambitions."

"I only want to help you."

"You're a liar," she said quietly. "You don't give a shit about me or anyone else. You just want to take it back.

These things have acid for blood where you Company people just have money. I don't see a lot of difference.''

Bishop II studied the floor for a moment before again raising his eyes to the solitary figure atop the crane platform. ''You have plenty of reasons to be wary, but unfortunately not much time. We just want to take you home. We don't care anymore what happens to it. We know what you've been through. You've shown great courage.''

''Bullshit!''

''You're wrong. We want to help.''

''What does that mean?''

''We want to take the thing out of you.''

''And keep it?''

Bishop II shook his head. ''No. Destroy it.''

She stood, swaying, wanting to believe him. Sensing her hesitation, he hurried on. ''Ripley, you're exhausted, worn out. Give yourself a moment. Stop and think. I have only your best interests at heart. The ship I came in, the *Patna*, is equipped with a state-of-the-art surgical facility. We can remove the fetus, or larva, or whatever you want to call it. We don't have a name for the different developmental stages yet. The operation will be successful! You're going to have a long, productive life.''

She looked down at him, calm now, resigned. ''I've had a life, thanks. One I didn't have to ask anybody about or answer to anybody for.''

He held up a hand, imploring. ''You're not thinking straight, Ripley! We admit we made mistakes. We didn't know. But we can make it up to you. All the potential lost, all the time. You can still have children. We'll buy out your contract. You'll get everything you deserve. We owe you.''

She wavered. ''You're not going to take it back?''

''No. We realize now what we've been up against.

You've been right all along. But time is running out. Let us deal with it. The surgery on the ship is ready to go."

The biotech immediately behind him stepped forward. "It's very quick. Painless. A couple of incisions. You'll be out for two hours—that's all. Then back on your feet, good as new. Whole again."

"What guarantee do I have that once you've taken this thing out you'll destroy it?"

Bishop II advanced another step. He was quite close now, looking across at her. "You're just going to have to trust me." He extended his hand in friendship. "Trust me. Please. We only want to help you."

She considered, taking her time. She saw Aaron watching her, and Morse. Her gaze went back to Bishop II.

She slid shut the gate between them. "No—"

A nod to Morse and he hit the control panel, putting the crane in motion. It rumbled away from the stairs, out over the furnace. As it did so, Bishop II lunged, grabbing at Ripley. She broke free and stumbled away from him.

The commandos responded and Morse took a bullet in the shoulder, dropping down behind the crane's control panel.

Aaron picked up a chunk of broken pipe, muttering, "You fucking droid!" The pipe landed hard on Bishop II's head.

The impact was spongy. Then man staggered, twitching, as his troops shot the acting superintendent down. Real blood poured from Bishop II's cracked skull.

"I am . . . not a . . . droid," the bleeding figure mumbled in surprise as it crumpled to the floor.

Ripley clutched at her chest. "It's moving." Company men rushed to the fallen Bishop II. He turned on his side, watching her.

"You owe it to us. You owe it to yourself."

A beatific smile crossed her face. Then she almost

snarled. "No way!" The crane platform was now directly over the caldron. Her stomach thumped and she staggered. Calmly, in complete control, she stepped to the edge. Below her feet boiled a lake of molten metal, the proximate inferno raising blisters on her skin, rising tendrils of heat reaching up invitingly.

"It's too late!"

"It's not!" Bishop II pleaded with her.

Staggering, she clutched both hands to her chest over the rising heat.

"Good-bye."

"Nooo!" Bishop II howled.

She stepped off the platform and vanished into the bubbling caldron below.

Morse had staggered erect in time to see her fall. Clutching at his wounded shoulder, he watched, murmuring.

"Those who are dead are not dead. They have moved up. Moved higher."

Having nothing else to do now, the biotechs bandaged Morse up. Other Company men, silent, not talking even among themselves, went about the business of methodically shutting down the furnace, the refinery, the rest of Weyland-Yutani Work Correctional Facility Fury 161.

Out *there* messages linger. Ghosts of radio transmissions drifting forever, echoes of words preceding and lives gone before. Occasionally they're detected, picked up, transcribed. Sometimes they mean something to those who hear; other times not. Sometimes they're lengthy, other times brief. As in . . .

"This is Ripley, last surviving member of the *Nostromo*, signing off."